CHILDREN'S DISCIPLESHIP SERIES | BOOK 1

Beginning the Christian Adventure

Bill Bright
Joette Whims and Melody Hunskor

NewLife
PUBLICATIONS

Beginning the Christian Adventure
Children's Discipleship Series, Book 1

Published by
NewLife **Publications**
A ministry of Campus Crusade for Christ
P.O. Box 620877
Orlando, FL 32862-0877

Edited by Lynn Copeland
Design and production by Genesis Group
Illustrations by Bruce Day
Cover by David Marty Design

Printed in the United States of America

ISBN 1-56399-151-9

Unless indicated otherwise, Scripture quotations are from the *New International Version,* © 1973, 1978, 1984 by the International Bible Society. Published by Zondervan Bible Publishers, Grand Rapids, Michigan.

Scripture quotations designated TLB are from *The Living Bible,* © 1971 by Tyndale House Publishers, Inc., Wheaton, Illinois.

Scripture quotations designated NLT are from the *New Living Translation,* © 1996 by Tyndale House Publishers, Inc., Wheaton, Illinois.

Scripture quotations designated NKJ are from the *New King James* version, © 1979, 1980, 1982 by Thomas Nelson Inc., Publishers, Nashville, Tennessee.

For more information, write:
Campus Crusade for Christ International—100 Lake Hart Drive, Orlando, FL 32832, USA
L.I.F.E., Campus Crusade for Christ—P.O. Box 40, Flemington Markets, 2129, Australia
Campus Crusade for Christ of Canada—Box 529, Sumas, WA 98295
Campus Crusade for Christ—Fairgate House, King's Road, Tyseley, Birmingham, B11 2AA, United Kingdom
Lay Institute for Evangelism, Campus Crusade for Christ—P.O. Box 8786, Auckland, 1035, New Zealand
Campus Crusade for Christ—9 Lock Road #3-03, PacCan Centre, Singapore
Great Commission Movement of Nigeria—P.O. Box 500, Jos, Plateau State, Nigeria, West Africa

Contents

Unit One: Who Is Jesus?

Unit Two: The Christian Adventure

Unit Three: Passport to a Joyful Life

Why a Discipleship Series for Children?

Our children are our greatest assets. In God's eyes, they are a heritage and a reward (Psalm 127:3). Whether you are a parent or a children's teacher, these preteens are the most vital resource you will ever have the privilege to touch.

Proverbs gives us the promise I am sure you have heard many times, "Train a child in the way he should go, and when he is old he will not turn from it" (22:6). What is God's method of training children? It is not to sit the child down and merely lecture him. God's method is a teach-as-you-go process. Before the Israelites entered the Promised Land, God instructed them how to teach their children His Word:

> Hear, O Israel! The LORD is our God, the LORD alone. And you must love the LORD your God with all your heart, all your soul, and all your strength. And you must commit yourselves wholeheartedly to these commands I am giving you today. Repeat them again and again to your children. Talk about them when you are at home and when you are away on a journey, when you are lying down and when you are getting up again. Tie them to your hands as a reminder, and wear them on your forehead. Write them on the doorposts of your house and on your gates (Deuteronomy 6:4–9, NLT).

The biblical pattern for learning is twofold: (1) children learn by watching, so adults must practice what they teach their children, by committing themselves wholeheartedly to God's commands; and (2) children learn by doing, by walking alongside a godly adult who lovingly and consistently guides them. This kind of teaching is deeply rooted in God's Word.

Children do best with active learning methods. The active learning method is basically what Jesus used in discipling His followers while He lived on this earth. Jesus not only preached to the crowds and taught through stories, He also emphasized all the truths He taught through example. The disciples saw how their Master patiently responded even when He was hungry and tired. They watched Him tenderly minister as the crowds pushed and shoved around Him. Their troubled hearts were soothed by His compassion, and their wrong attitudes received His gentle rebuke. They learned through situations they could see and touch, such as distributing the miraculously multiplied loaves of bread, experiencing a roaring sea become calm, and watching the diseased become whole. This was so much more effective for them than if they had simply heard Jesus say, "I can do anything." In the most moving demonstration of God's love, the disciples witnessed the horror of the crucifixion, which magnified the triumph and joy of the resurrection. Whatever Jesus taught, He lived and demonstrated to His disciples.

The Beginnings of the Series

Preteens are at a vulnerable time in their lives. They are changing rapidly. Your 9- and 10-year-old students may still regard you as a hero, whereas your 11- and 12-year-olds may question your authority. But this age is still relatively peaceful compared to the physical, emotional, and mental tumult these children will experience during their teen years. The preteen years are a marvelous time to give children a foundation in God's Word that they can use as they develop into adults.

The lessons in this book will help you harness the curiosity your students have about life. Your students are still young enough to enjoy the activities, but old enough to begin grasping some of the deeper and more abstract concepts of the Christian life.

The adult version of this material, *Ten Basic Steps Toward Christian Maturity*, has been used successfully around the world. The development of the Bible study series was a product of necessity. As the ministry of Campus Crusade for Christ expanded from the UCLA campus to scores of campuses across America, thousands of students committed their lives to Christ—several hundred on a single campus. A resource was needed to help them grow in their newfound faith.

In 1955, I asked several of my fellow staff to assist me in preparing Bible studies that would encourage both evangelism and spiritual growth in new believers. These studies would stimulate individuals and groups to explore the depths and riches of God's Word. *Ten Basic Steps Toward Christian Maturity* was the fruit of our combined labor.

Over the years since then, many believers have expressed a desire to teach these same biblical principles to their children. Some even adapted the adult version to do just that. They found that the basic principles taught in the adult series translated well to 9- to 12-year-olds.

Of course, discipling children is much different than teaching adults. You cannot sit children down with a Bible and lead a Bible study with them. Children need hands-on activities that will help them comprehend biblical principles. They need concrete examples and specific directions on how to apply the teachings to their life. This discipleship series was designed with their needs in mind.

How to Use the Series

This series of four books presents the basic doctrines and teachings of God's Word in a format that will attract your upper-elementary students. The books in this series can be used in two ways:

1. If you are going through the complete series, your students will begin with this book, *Beginning the Christian Adventure,* in which they will learn who Jesus is and how they can experience the life that Jesus has provided for each believer. The succeeding three books will teach:

   - *Discovering Our Awesome God*—Who God is and how He relates to us through His Holy Spirit

- *Growing in God's Word*—A basic overview of the Bible and how to study it for Christian growth

- *Building an Active Faith*—How to grow as a believer, including the importance of giving our whole selves to God, witnessing of His work in our life, and obeying Him

Each book will cover one-quarter of the year, and the complete series provides 52 lessons. By completing all four books, your students will have a well-rounded view of the Christian life.

2. Each book in the series is also designed to be used on its own. If you are not going on to the other three books, you will find that the units are complete in themselves.

This book begins with a lesson for the children's video *The Story of Jesus,* which you can use as an introductory lesson if desired. (See the Resources at the end of this book for information on ordering *The Story of Jesus* video.) The video is an adaptation of the *JESUS* film, an evangelistic tool that has been used around the world to introduce millions to Jesus.

I pray that these lessons will help you touch many children's lives for our Lord Jesus Christ. My prayer is that the upcoming generation will truly change our world for Christ!

How to Use the Lessons

Each lesson in this book is carefully crafted for an optimal learning experience. The lessons are built around several central themes:

- The *book objective* gives the overall purpose for the thirteen lessons.

- The *unit objective* defines how the unit will fit into the book's goal.

- The *lesson objective* shows what the learner will discover about God's message to us within the parameters of the book and unit goals.

- The *lesson application* describes what the learner should be able to do by the end of the lesson.

To accomplish the objectives and application, each lesson contains seven activities. Each builds on the previous activity to move the student to the application. Although the components may appear in different order, each lesson contains the following:

Opening Activity: Usually a more active part of the lesson, this activity will grab your students' attention and help them begin focusing on the upcoming lesson objective.

Bible Story: This story or Bible truth illustrates the main principle of the lesson. The story is presented in a way that will hold the attention of your students and engage them in the learning process. The Bible story develops the lesson objective.

Lesson Activity: This hands-on activity involves the students in discovering more about the truths presented in the Bible story. The activity helps students begin applying biblical truths to their daily life.

Check for Understanding: This is a short review of what the students learned, to help you assess their progress and what you might need to re-emphasize.

Memory Verse Activity: This fun activity will help your students memorize the central Bible verse of the lesson.

Application: This lesson component will challenge your students to apply what they have learned to specific situations in their lives. The application is directly related to the lesson objective.

Weekly Assignment: Because the purpose of this series is discipleship, the concluding component of the lesson will encourage students to use the lesson application during the week to help them begin developing biblical spiritual habits. At the beginning of the succeeding lesson, the students will discuss how they completed the weekly assignment.

Try to enlist the aid of the parents by explaining about the weekly assignments and what they will do for each child. If possible, explain this when the parents come to drop off or pick up the student, or call them after the first lesson. Some children without a good support system at home may find it difficult to follow through on the weekly assignments. If you have students who do not have support at home, consider meeting with them individually to encourage them and help them grow spiritually. They will also benefit from hearing about other students' experiences. Therefore, make your first activity of the lesson a discussion time about the weekly assignment.

Lesson Structure

The lessons are written to include about an hour's worth of activities. However, you can adapt the material to an hour and fifteen minutes or an hour and a half.

The point of these lesson segments is not to slavishly follow the suggestions given for you. Adapt the lessons to your teaching style without changing the purpose for each component.

The most important aspect of active learning is the debriefing portion of each activity. This debriefing usually involves discussion questions that relate the activity to Scripture and to the lesson objective. Therefore, it is essential to allow enough time during each lesson segment to talk about the activity. If you find that the activities are taking longer than the allotted time, it is better to shorten a later activity than to skip the debriefing questions. If your activities are running short, add questions such as these:

- What will you do differently this week because of what you learned today?

- What feelings did you have during our activity? Why did you have this reaction?

- What was the most important thing you learned? Why was it the most important to you?

- How was the experience of the person in the Bible story like experiences we might have today? How would you have reacted in a similar situation?

As you teach, encourage your students to be risk-takers in what they express. This will require that you treat each person's response with respect. It will also involve listening to what your students say and allowing plenty of time for responses. During this time, assess where your students are spiritually regarding the point of the activity. This discussion will also give you opportunities to talk over many important matters with your students. You may be the only person who can give some students a biblical perspective on life issues. Their responses will help you direct the remainder of the lesson to fit your students' needs.

Most of the debriefing questions are open-ended and require thoughtful answers. Provided after the questions are responses your students are likely to give. If the students' answers seem off-track, help refocus the discussion by restating the question in different words or suggesting a more appropriate response.

The lessons use these conventions to help you follow the lesson structure:

Bold text: instructions to the teacher

Normal text: guided conversation for teaching

- Bulleted questions: questions for classroom discussion

(Italic text in parentheses): possible answers to questions

Gathering Supplies

The Lesson Plan at the beginning of each lesson lists the supplies you will need. Many are items found in typical church classrooms. The lessons assume that the classroom will have a chalkboard and chalk.

Be sure to read and prepare the lesson thoroughly. Some activities may require prior preparation.

Make sure each student has a Bible of his or her own. Encourage students to look up the Bible story as you tell it and to find the memory verse reference. Ask students to read short passages used in the activities, but avoid calling on children to read whose reading skills lag behind others in the group. If you have nonreaders, pair these students with good readers when doing reading activities.

The following rule is essential to keep in mind when teaching children: *The lessons are for the students, not the students for the lessons.* Make sure your students are your priority, not getting through the lesson in a certain way. And have fun learning together!

The Exciting World of the 9- to 12-Year-Old

In some ways, your students live in a world of their own. As teachers, we can never fully understand what they are going through or how they think. But our challenge is to understand them as well as we can and use our knowledge to help them grow mentally, emotionally, socially, physically, and most of all, spiritually. Each child is an individual with unique problems and talents. Each will be at a different place in his or her spiritual journey. At the same time, they will all be affected by similar growing and maturing forces and environments. Keep in mind that their lack of maturity in other areas will affect how they grow spiritually.

If you have previously taught children in this age group, you probably understand how much they are developing in all areas of their lives. The following guidelines will help you see where the student is:

Mental Development
> Moving from literal toward abstract thinking
> Increasing concentration length
> Beginning to understand the significance of past and future but still concerned with the here-and-now
> Creative and curious
> Well-developed problem-solving skills
> Able to think critically

Emotional Development
> Alternating between acting responsibly and childishly
> More self-directed and independent
> Sometimes fears bad situations like parents' divorce or being a victim of violence

Social Development
> Peer-oriented but still looks to adults for guidance
> Relates better with same-sex friends
> Likes having one best friend
> May act in socially inappropriate ways
> Enjoys group activities

Physical Development
> Lots of energy
> Girls may be taller and more coordinated than boys

Likes a variety of activities
Is good with fine motor skills

Spiritual Development
Is developing a value system and a conscience
Can put into practice Bible teachings
Has a clear sense of right and wrong, of fair and unfair
Eager to trust Jesus
Able to make choices and follow through

To help your students build a value system based on God's Word, you will have to move them beyond merely acquiring knowledge to applying biblical truths. The learning process includes these five progressive steps:

1. Feeling

2. Knowing

3. Understanding

4. Applying

5. Practicing

Each lesson is set up to explore your students' feelings about the topic, introduce Bible knowledge, help them apply what they learn, and begin practicing the application on a consistent basis. Each component of the lesson is designed to help move your students through the five progressive steps to making the spiritual concepts part of their lives.

As you teach these lessons, enjoy the world of your students. Do the activities with them. Play the games. Memorize the verse. Enter into the excitement of the activities and the joy of discovering our great and wonderful God. Your journey in discipling children can be just as valuable as theirs will be.

Tips for Teaching Your Students

Each teacher has his or her own style that makes a classroom run well. However, a few basic tips can help you utilize your teaching methods in a more effective manner. The following are suggestions you can use to augment your teaching:

- *Get to know your students.* Every child wants to know that the adults in his life are aware of him and his needs. Begin by calling each student by name. Make a prayer list that includes all your students and keep it up-to-date. Keep track of each student's needs, problems, and talents. Treat each child as an individual.

- *Make your classroom a "safe" zone.* Students at this age can be cruel and thoughtless. Learning skills can be difficult for some students. Other students will have a hard time interacting with children their age. You can help by making sure that each child is treated with respect in your classroom. Praise everyone's accomplishments—even if they do not seem very accomplished to you. Compliment a child who has trouble memorizing when he shows progress. Make a game easier for a child who has poor coordination. And make sure no one in your classroom makes unkind remarks about anyone else. Your "safe" classroom will help students open up during discussion times and feel welcome and comfortable.

- *Look for creative ways to use the available space.* Often we use classroom space the same way all the time. Look around your classroom. Could you move furniture to make the activities work better? Is there space in a fellowship hall, a lobby, or outdoors that would work well for games? Is your classroom big enough to divide into sections for different activities? Can you reserve a corner for discussion and decorate it accordingly?

- *Keep the lesson moving.* Children have a short attention span. They will lose interest if you are not prepared or if you use a slow pace. If students get bored with a game or activity, move on to the debriefing questions.

- *Be aware of your students' moods, personalities, and family situations.* Some days, children will bound into your room talking and ready to go. Other days, it will seem as if you cannot get anyone to respond. An incident during the week may affect a student's behavior. For example, a student whose parents have recently separated may be especially withdrawn or unruly. Learn to recognize the behavior that tells you something is wrong with that child. Keep all your students in prayer for all their needs and concerns.

- *Use consistent discipline with your students.* Write your classroom rules on poster board and post them in your classroom. Then follow the rules. Avoid reprimanding any child in the presence of others. Also, teach your students a signal to get their attention. You might flash the lights on and off or raise your hand for silence. Practice the attention-getting signal until your students obey it. Despite your best efforts, your class will probably have at least one student who will test your patience. As a last resort, you may have to remove an unruly child from the room. Before you begin teaching, work out discipline procedures for unruly students with another adult such as your children's department leader or pastor.

- *Use different teaching styles.* Children, like adults, learn best in different ways. Some are visual learners and learn best when they see things. Others are auditory learners and learn best by hearing. Still others are kinesthetic learners who function best by touching. The lessons are geared to use all types of learning styles, but be aware of how each child learns best so you can help all your students get the most out of the lessons.

- *Be open to adjusting your lesson if the moment warrants.* At times, you will find your students especially open to discussing important topics that the lesson does not cover. Take advantage of these moments to talk with them. Sometimes, an activity will fail to go as planned. When that happens, adjust your debriefing questions to facilitate learning even more. For example, if you were doing an activity with a balloon and the balloon popped before you could finish, you might turn your lesson into an example of how to react when things do not go right.

- *Plan for early arrivers.* Some students will arrive early. Be prepared with activities they can do. One suggestion is to make an ongoing bulletin board that relates to the lesson. For example, the first unit uses a newspaper called *Sonshine Jerusalem News*. Create a bulletin board around that theme. Set out articles from your local newspaper that give religious news and have early arrivers put them on the bulletin board. Have students write questions people may have about Jesus on slips of paper and post them. Discuss these questions at an appropriate point during the unit. Put up a "play bill" of the characters in your skit and the "actors" who played each character.

You might ask students to arrange chairs, set out supplies, or work on an activity sheet that goes along with the lesson theme. Another idea is to bring a mailbox with a flag that you can set up in your classroom. Set out slips of paper and pencils. The first student can choose to write a prayer request and put it in the mailbox. He then raises the mailbox flag. As other students come in, they too can write prayer requests and put them in the mailbox. Then sometime during the lesson, use the "mailed" prayer requests for a class prayer time.

- *Use "after class" moments wisely.* Most of your students will be anxious to leave once the lesson is over. Elementary students tend to begin anticipating the next event before the current one ends. But occasionally a student will hang back. Some students enjoy relating to a teacher and may frequently stay behind. Other students may have parents who are involved in other ministries in your church and have been asked to remain in the classroom until they can be picked up. Rather than resenting the extra time children spend in your classroom, plan for these possibilities.

Allow students to help you straighten up the classroom and begin preparing for the next lesson. They could gather supplies, help you photocopy handouts, or do simple cutting preparations. While you work, discuss what they learned during the day's activities.

Use this time to develop a deeper relationship with the students who linger behind. Over the course of a few months, you may end up spending extra time with most of your students. Preteens will open up to you more easily if you talk to them naturally while you are working together on a project. Occasionally, a student may hang back out of a desire to talk about a crisis in his or her life. If necessary, ask for help from the staff in your children's department.

Another "after class" idea is to have students help you plan and put on a reception for their parents. This will help you meet the parents and understand them better. This reception will work well either near the beginning or near the end of the unit. Make sure you send home announcements for the two weeks prior to the reception. Since the event is for the parents, plan simple refreshments that either your children's department can provide or that a few volunteers can supply. Present a Certificate of Completion to each student for completing this Bible study.

God bless you as you reach the newest generation for our Lord Jesus Christ!

The Story of Jesus

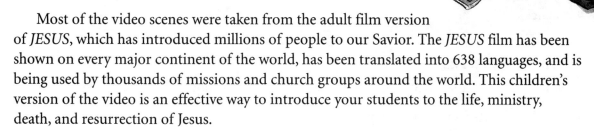

The video *The Story of Jesus for Children* is designed to show children of all ages the true story of Jesus as adapted from the Gospel of Luke. The video will introduce your students to the life of Jesus through a format that they understand well—moving pictures and sound.

Most of the video scenes were taken from the adult film version of *JESUS*, which has introduced millions of people to our Savior. The *JESUS* film has been shown on every major continent of the world, has been translated into 638 languages, and is being used by thousands of missions and church groups around the world. This children's version of the video is an effective way to introduce your students to the life, ministry, death, and resurrection of Jesus.

You may wish to show this video before you begin your Children's Discipleship Series lessons. During the first unit in the series, "Who Is Jesus?," your students will learn about who Jesus is and what He has done for us. The video can serve as a dynamic introduction to the lesson material as well as an evangelistic tool for those students who have never received Jesus as their Savior. Units 2 and 3 build on this introduction to Jesus by showing your students how to begin their Christian adventure.

The video is 62 minutes long. If your class periods are one hour or less, you may choose to show the video over two sessions. The following chart gives two lesson plans you can use to fit the program you are offering for your students.

NUMBER OF SESSIONS	TIME NEEDED	LESSON PLAN
1	70 to 90 minutes	• Introduce the video • View the entire video • Allow for response from the video
2	45 to 60 minutes	• Introduce the video • View the video up to the events of the crucifixion • View the rest of the video • Allow for response from the video

Note: To fit this study into a yearly quarter of 13 lessons, begin with the single-lesson video presentation and omit Lesson 13 (the review lesson).

Lesson Materials

To view the video, you will need to obtain the following:

- A copy of the video *The Story of Jesus for Children* (See Resources to order.)

- A VCR/TV

- A copy of the booklet *The Greatest Promise* for each student (See Resources to order.)

- A copy of a Promise Card for each student (A reproducible page is provided at the end of this lesson.)

- Pencils

Lesson Objectives

As you prepare for the video lesson, keep in mind the following lesson objectives:

- To show students the true story of Jesus

- To allow students to see and understand the promises of God through His Son Jesus

- To give every student who views the video an opportunity to voluntarily choose to ask Jesus to live in them

LESSON PLAN

OPENING ACTIVITY: Introduce the Video

Before Class: Cue the video. Gather your students around the TV. To begin, give the following brief history of the video.

About 2,000 years ago, Jesus of Nazareth was born in Bethlehem. He was God's Son sent to earth. He said, "If you have seen Me, you know what God is like." He also said, "I have come to do God's will on earth." Because He is God, what He said and how He lived and died is the most important story we'll ever hear. How Jesus lived and what He taught is the standard we must use to measure right from wrong.

The video we will see is called *The Story of Jesus for Children.* Some of you may have seen parts of this video in your church or school or perhaps even on television. Let me give you some facts about the video.

1. Scenes from the original film were done in the nation of Israel as close as possible to where the original events took place 2,000 years ago.

2. Dozens of experts such as historians, archaeologists, and theologians worked for five years doing research to make sure the film was accurate.

3. In the video, Jesus speaks only the words recorded in the Gospel of Luke from God's book, the Bible.

The children in this video are actors. The parts they play are only a story. The children's story is not found in the Bible. The reason the video presents a children's story along with the story of Jesus is to help you understand what is happening. We do not know how children interacted with Jesus while He was on earth. We do know that Jesus loved children very much. But the facts about Jesus and what He did and said are true. The children's story may have happened something like this . . .

LESSON ACTIVITY: Show the Video

Show the video all the way to the end. The video is not over after the last dramatic scene. The last part of the video gives your students an opportunity to invite Jesus to live in them.

APPLICATION: Allow for Responses

When the video is finished, hand out the Promise Cards and pencils. Say: Please write your name, address, and telephone number on the Promise Card. Then check the boxes to tell your ideas about what you have said, thought, or done as you watched the video.

Distribute *The Greatest Promise* booklets when appropriate. This booklet is yours to take home and read with your family and friends. If you have made a decision to invite Jesus into your life, come and tell me after I dismiss our class.

Close in prayer, thanking God for sending Jesus to die for us. You may want to introduce the unit on Jesus before you dismiss your students.

Collect the cards and quickly note the boxes each student checked. Make yourself available to talk to students who indicated that they asked Jesus to come into their lives. Read through *The Greatest Promise* booklet with students who have questions about their relationship with God. You may want to ask other adults who are experienced children's teachers to help you with this counseling.

Promise Card
(Commitment Card)

☐ I prayed today and asked Jesus to live in me.

☐ I already asked Jesus to live in me.

☐ I am not ready to ask Jesus into my life.

☐ I would like to learn more about Jesus.

NAME: _____

ADDRESS: _____

_____

CITY: _____

STATE: _____   ZIP: _____

☐ BOY   ☐ GIRL   AGE: _____

PHONE: _____

Give to your teacher or parent.

Promise Card
(Commitment Card)

☐ I prayed today and asked Jesus to live in me.

☐ I already asked Jesus to live in me.

☐ I am not ready to ask Jesus into my life.

☐ I would like to learn more about Jesus.

NAME: _____

ADDRESS: _____

_____

CITY: _____

STATE: _____   ZIP: _____

☐ BOY   ☐ GIRL   AGE: _____

PHONE: _____

Give to your teacher or parent.

My Prayer

Today I prayed this prayer:

Dear God,

I believe Jesus is Your Son. Thank You that Jesus died on the cross for all the wrong things I have thought and said and done. Please forgive me for my sins. I ask Jesus to be with me and to live in me always. Help me to be the kind of person You want me to be. Thank You for answering my prayer. Amen.

NAME: _____

DATE: _____

Keep in your Bible.

My Prayer

Today I prayed this prayer:

Dear God,

I believe Jesus is Your Son. Thank You that Jesus died on the cross for all the wrong things I have thought and said and done. Please forgive me for my sins. I ask Jesus to be with me and to live in me always. Help me to be the kind of person You want me to be. Thank You for answering my prayer. Amen.

NAME: _____

DATE: _____

Keep in your Bible.

Jesus and Me Every Day

When you ask Jesus to forgive you and invite Him to be with you, He really is with you now and always. He always keeps His promises. In the Bible Jesus makes many promises to help you be certain about your relationship with Him. Here are two of His promises:

"I am with you always." *(Matthew 28:20)*
"I will never leave you." *(Hebrews 13:5)*

As you begin this new life with God and His Son, Jesus, God will help you make the right choices. Here is another promise from God's book, the Bible:

"God is working in you to help you want to do what pleases Him. Then He gives you the power to do it." *(Philippians 2:13)*

(Bible verses from *International Children's Bible*)

Jesus and Me Every Day

When you ask Jesus to forgive you and invite Him to be with you, He really is with you now and always. He always keeps His promises. In the Bible Jesus makes many promises to help you be certain about your relationship with Him. Here are two of His promises:

"I am with you always." *(Matthew 28:20)*
"I will never leave you." *(Hebrews 13:5)*

As you begin this new life with God and His Son, Jesus, God will help you make the right choices. Here is another promise from God's book, the Bible:

"God is working in you to help you want to do what pleases Him. Then He gives you the power to do it." *(Philippians 2:13)*

(Bible verses from *International Children's Bible*)

Who Is Jesus?

BOOK OBJECTIVE	To introduce students to Jesus and the Christian life and to help them begin to grow as believers.
UNIT OBJECTIVE	To help students appropriate the life-giving power and pardon of Jesus in their lives.
LESSON 1: Perfect Predictions	*Objective:* To help students learn that the fulfillment of Old Testament prophecies about Jesus proves that He is the Son of God. *Application:* To challenge students to believe that Jesus is the Son of God.
LESSON 2: Powerful Proof	*Objective:* To help students learn that Jesus proved that He was the Son of God through the power of the things He did. *Application:* To help students make a prayer pact in which they record how Jesus powerfully answers their prayers.
LESSON 3: Resurrection Power	*Objective:* To help students learn that Jesus died on the cross to pay for the sins they have committed. *Application:* To challenge students to become members of God's family or to share their faith with others.
LESSON 4: Gracious Savior	*Objective:* To help students recognize Christ's power to overcome problems in their lives. *Application:* To help students examine their lives to commit problem areas to Christ's control.

No other person in history has influenced the world for good more than Jesus Christ. His life and message have greatly changed the lives of people and nations. History is His Story, the story of the life of one Man. Remove Jesus of Nazareth from history, and it would be a completely different account. Indeed, there has never been anyone who could compare with Jesus. He is unique among all human beings.

Charles Spurgeon, an English theologian, wrote:

> Christ is the central fact in the world's history. To him everything looks forward or backward. All the lines of history converge upon him. All the great purposes of God cul-

minate in him. The greatest and most momentous fact that the history of the world records is the fact of his birth.[1]

Jesus has influenced the whole world. Consider today's date on your calendar. It gives witness to the fact that Jesus of Nazareth, the Christ, lived on this earth. "B.C." means "before Christ"; "A.D." is the abbreviation of *anno Domini*, a Latin phrase that is translated "in the year of our Lord." His followers have made a difference in civilization in areas such as social reform, medicine, business practices, science, law and government, arts and culture, and education. If you examine the roots of most of our good social practices, you will find them going back to the principles that Jesus taught.

People sometimes ask me, "Is Christianity really established on historical facts?" When I talk about Christ to great scholars today, I am appalled to find that many of them do not believe Jesus is the Son of God, our Savior. Nearly always, these men are ignorant of the basic truths of the gospel. They take issue with something that they do not fully understand. As we talked and reasoned together, these scholars have been honest in confessing, "I have not taken the time to read the Bible or to consider the historical facts concerning Jesus." But I have yet to meet a person who has honestly considered the overwhelming evidence proving the deity of Jesus of Nazareth who does not admit that He is the Son of God.

Tragically, in our world many try to influence our young people to consider Christ as just a "good man" or a "great teacher." And that He certainly was not the Son of God.

This unit will introduce your students to Jesus and help them see how He proved Himself to be God's Son, sent to save the world of its sin. The facts your students learn will enable them to anchor their faith onto biblical truth rather than flimsy worldly thinking. Your students will also be challenged to receive Christ as Savior and become part of God's family. They will learn how to appropriate Christ's resurrection power in their prayer lives.

This life-changing spiritual birth will enable your students to begin their Christian adventure. In the next few weeks, your preteens will learn the difference Christ can make in a person's life and how to grow in their new life in Christ.

At some point in this unit, share with your students your testimony of how you became a Christian. Make your testimony simple and short to keep their attention. Write out what you want to say if necessary and practice it before class. Time yourself to make sure your testimony does not last more than two minutes. Your faith in Christ will make more of an impact on your students' beliefs than any other part of the lesson you teach.

---

1 Sherwood Eliot Wirt and Kersten Beckstrom, *Living Quotations for Christians* (New York: Harper & Row Publishers, 1974), No. 1749.

Perfect Predictions

LESSON PLAN

OBJECTIVE: Students will learn that the fulfillment of Old Testament prophecies about Jesus proves that He is the Son of God.

APPLICATION: Students will be challenged to believe that Jesus is the Son of God.

LESSON PLAN ELEMENT	ACTIVITY	TIME	SUPPLIES
Opening Activity	*Paper Predictions*	7–10	Can or box with lid; 20 4"×4" different-colored squares of paper (e.g., 5 red, 5 green, 5 yellow, 5 blue); paper; pencils
Bible Story—Assorted Scriptures about prophecies	*Strange Happenings Reported in Jerusalem*	10–15	Bibles; *Sonshine Jerusalem News* handouts; paper; pencils
Check for Understanding	*Picture What Happened*	5–7	*Sonshine Jerusalem News* handouts; pencils; markers
Lesson Activity	*I Knew Him!*	7–10	6 copies of "I Knew Him!" skit; microphone; optional props for skit (see activity for suggestions); tape recorder (optional)
Memory Verse Activity	*Whispers and Shouts*	3–5	Music for *He Is Lord*
Application	*Who Do You Say I Am?*	5–8	Bible; *Sonshine Jerusalem News* handouts; pencils; tape recorder
Weekly Assignment	*"Who Do You Say Jesus Is?" Survey*	3–5	"Who Do You Say Jesus Is?" Survey for each student

LESSON INTRODUCTION

What if you could predict that a major world event would take place five minutes from now? What if you could accurately describe future events? Would knowing the future give you unusual power?

Would anyone believe you? Possibly some would, but how many would not?

Many people do not believe the Bible, yet it miraculously foretells hundreds of events, sometimes in minute detail, and usually hundreds—sometimes thousands—of years ahead. Some prophecies concern cities and countries, such as Tyre, Jericho, Samaria, Jerusalem, Palestine, Moab, and Babylon. Others relate to specific individuals. Many have already been fulfilled, but some are still in the future.

Jesus Christ is the subject of more than 300 Old Testament prophecies. His birth 2,000 years ago and events of His life were foretold by many prophets spanning a period of 1,500 years. History confirms that even the smallest detail happened just as predicted. These prophets confirm beyond a doubt that Jesus is the true Messiah, the Son of God, and Savior of the world.

The following chart lists some of the amazing predictions concerning Jesus Christ. This week, read these Bible passages and meditate on the reliability of the predictions of Jesus' birth, life, death, and resurrection. Ask God how you can best relate that truth to your students.

BIBLICAL PREDICTIONS AND FULFILLMENT		
EVENT	**OLD TESTAMENT PROPHECY**	**FULFILLMENT IN JESUS**
His birth	Isaiah 7:14	Matthew 1:18,22,23
His birthplace	Micah 5:2	Matthew 2:4,6,7
His childhood in Egypt	Hosea 1:1	Matthew 2:14,15
The purpose for His death	Isaiah 53:4–6	2 Corinthians 5:21; 1 Peter 2:24
His betrayal	Zechariah 11:12,13; 13:6	Matthew 26:14–16; 27:3–10
His crucifixion	Psalm 22	Matthew 27
His resurrection	Psalm 16:9,10	Acts 2:31

When you finish, read the claims Jesus made about Himself: Mark 14:61,62; John 5:17,18; 6:38; 8:42; 10:30.

Jesus claimed to be God. He made the kinds of claims that only a person who presumed He was God would make. Both His friends and His enemies called Him God, and He never attempted to deny it. He even commended His followers for believing He was God. One of the essential beliefs of the Christian life is that Jesus is truly God in the flesh.

To prepare your heart for this lesson, prayerfully answer the following questions:

- Who do you think Jesus is and on what do you base that belief? List facts which particularly help you know that He is God.

- Why is it important that you personally recognize who Jesus Christ really is?

- What changes have you experienced in your life as a result of receiving Him as your Savior and Lord?

DING!
DONG!

OPENING ACTIVITY: Paper Predictions

Put the paper squares into the can (or box) and put the lid on. Set the can in front of the class. Pass out pencils and paper to your students. Write the following chart on your chalkboard. Ask students to draw the chart on their papers.

	YOUR PREDICTION	CORRECT ANSWER
WHAT IS IN THE CAN?	1. 2.	
COLOR PREDICTION	3. 4. 5. 6.	

Point to the can. Do you think you are a good guesser? Do you think you can predict what is in this can? Write your prediction on your chart beside #1. **Give students a few moments to write their predictions. Then have several students give their predictions aloud.** You knew that this box couldn't contain things like a refrigerator or a car. They are too large to fit inside this can. You had to write down something smaller than that. **Shake the box, and allow the students to lift it and shake it also.**

- Does the sound change your prediction? *(Yes, maybe.)*

The more we know and experience, the better we can make a more accurate prediction. Write another prediction beside #2 on your chart. **Give students another moment to write a prediction under #2. Then have several give their predictions aloud.**

Open the can and show the contents to the students. Now predict which color square will be drawn from the can. Write your prediction beside the next number. **Have students write a color beside #3, then have one student draw a square from the can. Have students write the correct answer for #3. Repeat for numbers 4, 5, and 6. When finished, discuss how many times students guessed right or wrong.**

These color predictions were easy to make because we had only four options to choose from.

- What do you think would happen if we had one hundred different choices? *(We wouldn't get any right. We would have too many choices to guess right.)*

Imagine what would happen if you had to guess the future. No one can really predict what's going to happen in the future. Even if we know what we plan to do tomorrow, things may happen to change our plans.

- What one thing happened yesterday that caused you to change your plans? *(My mom got sick so we couldn't go shopping. A good TV program came on so I forgot to call my friend.)*

No one could have predicted the day he was born or the day he will die. As people, we are not very good predictors. The newspaper can't predict when a disaster like an earthquake will happen. The television newscasters can't tell us what will happen either. They can only make guesses. But God can tell us what is going to happen in the future. He knows everything. Even before He made the world, He planned to send His Son, Jesus Christ, to the earth. He told men who were called prophets about these plans. In the Old Testament, the prophets wrote about Jesus' coming. The prophets called Him the Messiah, which means the "sent one." The prophets predicted how Jesus would be born, how He would live and die— 2,000 years before Jesus was born. The prophets predicted more than 300 things about Jesus. Every one of these predictions came true! Not one of them was wrong! That's how we know that Jesus is the true Messiah, the Son of God, and the Savior of the world!

In our lesson, we're going to learn about these amazing predictions, and we'll also learn about the Messiah, the Person the prophets predicted would come.

BIBLE STORY: Strange Happenings Reported in Jerusalem!

Pass out a *Sonshine Jerusalem News* to each student. Ask students to look at the front page. During the time Jesus lived on earth, paper and printing presses had not yet been invented. There were no newspapers, televisions, or video cameras to report important events. News mostly traveled by one person talking to another person.

What do you think would have happened if the people who lived when Jesus was on earth would have had newspapers? What kind of headlines do you think Jesus' death would have made? Today, we're going to imagine that the *Sonshine Jerusalem News* was on the scene after Jesus rose from the dead. Let's see what people said about Him.

Divide students into five groups. Give each group a piece of paper and a pencil. Assign one person in each group as the reader and one as the reporter. Assign each group one of the pairs of Scripture references in the story. In each group, the reader will read the story to the group, then students will look up their group's verses and summarize what they say about Jesus. The reporter will write down their ideas. The Old Testament passages are the predictions and the New Testament passages are their fulfillment in Jesus. When groups are finished, reconvene as a class and have reporters tell about their group's verses. When reporters finish, ask the following questions:

- What do you think it felt like to be living in Jerusalem when all these things were happening? *(Exciting; I would have been scared.)*

- How could these prophets make predictions that always came true? *(Their words were from God. God was speaking through them.)*

- How does it make you feel to know that the Bible's predictions about Jesus all came true 100 percent? *(It helps me believe in Jesus. I feel good about trusting the Bible.)*

CHECK FOR UNDERSTANDING: Picture What Happened

Do you see that empty picture frame beside the newspaper article? We can be illustrators for the *Sonshine Jerusalem News.* Draw one part of the story of Jesus to go along with the article. For example, you could draw a picture of how Jesus was born in a stable, how He was betrayed by Judas, how He died on a cross, or how His tomb is now empty.

Pass out markers and give students a few minutes to complete their drawings. Then have them share what they drew with the rest of the class.

Living in Jerusalem when Jesus was on earth must have been an exciting experience. Many miraculous things happened. Right now, let's talk to some people who were on the scene during that time.

LESSON ACTIVITY: I Knew Him!

Teaching Tips: To make this activity more fun, ask an adult to videotape your skit, then play it for another class next week or for yourselves if you have time at the end of your class period. Stay within the allotted time limit in the lesson plan.

Bring small props for your students, such as cloths for headscarves, a play sword, a bathrobe, or a money bag for Zacchaeus. Write *Sonshine Jerusalem News* on half an index card and tape it to the microphone. If desired, bring a tape recorder and cassette tape for your reporter to use.

Choose good readers from your class to play the following roles:

Dan Rathernot, a reporter
Zacchaeus, a former tax collector
Martha, a friend of Jesus
Pilate, a Roman governor
Anthony, a Roman soldier
Thomas, a disciple of Jesus

Give each actor a copy of the skit. Have actors quickly review their parts so they can read them aloud during the interview. (The object of this activity is not to produce a well-acted script but just to get your students thinking about who Jesus is.) All other students will act as the crowd watching the reporter interview the skit characters.

Have the five people to be interviewed sit in chairs in front of the class. Instruct the reporter to stand in front of the interviewees and hold a microphone in front of each person as he or she reads from the script.

Have the students act out the skit by reading the parts and doing the actions. When the skit is finished, say: When Jesus was on earth, people had different opinions about who He was. But the people who knew Him best believed that He was and is God. Jesus' friends saw Him after He was raised from the dead. They saw Him go back to heaven on a cloud.

- What did Jesus do to prove He was God? *(Raised people from the dead; healed people; was raised from the dead Himself.)*

- What did Jesus' friends believe about Jesus? *(That He was God; that He came back to life.)*

- If someone asked you who you believe Jesus is, what would you say? *(He is God. He is my Savior. I'm not sure.)*

One of the most important things we can do is to believe that Jesus is God's only Son and that He came to earth to pay for our sins. He loves us so much that He was willing to die on a cross to pay for our sins. Our part is to believe that He is God's Son and that He paid for our sins. Then we can ask Him to forgive our sins and to be our Savior. When we do, we become part of God's family. We'll learn more about God's family in a later lesson.

> *Teaching Tip:* An alternate activity would be to have students one at a time give a fact from the lesson that proves Jesus is God (He rose from the dead, performed miracles, fulfilled prophecy, and so forth).

Right now, let's look at what God's Word says about Jesus.

MEMORY VERSE ACTIVITY: Whispers and Shouts
Philippians 2:11—"Every tongue [should] confess that Jesus Christ is Lord, to the glory of God the Father."

Write the verse on the chalkboard. Have your students sit in a circle. Read Philippians 2:11 to them. This verse explains that we should tell others that Jesus is Lord or God. When we do this, it brings glory or honor to God the Father. In our lesson today, we heard many different things that people said about Jesus. We heard the things that Jesus said about Himself—most importantly that He is God. We can also tell others about these things with our tongues. Let's do this by practicing this verse today. Turn to your neighbor and whisper, "Jesus is Lord!" **Give students time to do this.** Turn to another neighbor and shout, "Jesus is Lord!" **Give students time to do this.** Now let's all whisper together, "Jesus is Lord." **Lead your students in whispering, then say:** Let's all shout out loud together, "Jesus is Lord." **When finished, say:** Our words bring glory and honor to God the Father. It also brings glory and honor to God when we memorize His Word. Let's try to memorize this verse together.

Repeat the verse with your class several times. Give students a few minutes to practice or study the verse on their own. Would anyone care to come into the center of the circle and say this verse by memory? **Allow volunteers to say the verse. Finish by singing the chorus of *He Is Lord* or another song that emphasizes the lordship of Jesus Christ.**

APPLICATION: Who Do You Say I Am?

The Bible tells us that Jesus asked His disciples this question: "Who do you say that I am?" Peter answered immediately, "You are the Christ, the Son of the Living God." Jesus was very pleased with Peter's answer. **Read Matthew 16:13–17.**

What if you had been with the disciples that day? What would you have said if Jesus asked you, "Who do you say that I am?" Write or draw your answer on the back of your newspaper.

While the students are writing or drawing, pick a quiet area in the room and call students up one at a time to record on a tape recorder their verbal answer to the question: "Who do you say Jesus is?" Try to ask everyone in the class, if time permits. Then allow students who would like to share their drawings or written answers with the class to do so. Play back the recorded answers.

WEEKLY ASSIGNMENT: "Who Do You Say Jesus Is?" Survey

Distribute the "Who Do You Say Jesus Is?" Surveys.

Today we found out what many people said about Jesus. We discovered who Jesus said He was. We also learned what each person in our class felt about Jesus. This week, let's find out what people you know think about Jesus. Take this survey home and ask people the question, "Who do you say Jesus is? Is He God or is He not God?" Put a checkmark beside the answer that best fits the person's answer. Then ask the person the reason for their answer and write that in the last column. Bring your survey back next week and we will discuss them.

Close in prayer, thanking God for sending His Son, Jesus.

After class, review the tape-recorded responses from the individual students about who Jesus is. How your students answered this question will help you determine where they are in their spiritual life. Begin praying for each student and how you can help him or her have a deeper relationship with Jesus Christ. Pray especially for the ones you think may not have made a decision to follow Christ as Savior and Lord.

Testimony of
Roman Soldier

NEWS, page iv

WEATHER

● Blackout
at noon

Local Woman
Wins Bake-off

FOOD, page xix

SONSHINE
Jerusalem News

VOL. XI, ISS. IV   33 A.D.

Strange Happenings Reported in Jerusalem

JERUSALEM—Over the last few months, many strange things have been happening in Jerusalem. These things are all about one person—Jesus Christ. More than 500 witnesses say they saw Him alive after He died! The *Sonshine Jerusalem News* investigated the life and death of this man, Jesus. We found surprising evidence. Many people, who are called prophets, predicted how Jesus would be born and how He would die.

A prophet named Micah lived hundreds of years before Jesus was born. Yet he named the very place the Messiah would be born—Bethlehem. (Micah 5:2; Matthew 2:4,6,7) That's exactly what happened. Jesus Christ was born not too far from Jerusalem in the little town of Bethlehem. He was born in a stable because his parents, Joseph and Mary, couldn't find a room in an inn when they traveled to Bethlehem.

The prophet Hosea wrote that the Messiah would spend his early years in Egypt. (Hosea 1:1; Matthew 2:14,15) That's exactly what happened to Jesus. When He was just a child, His parents moved to Egypt and lived there for several years.

In the last three years of His life, crowds of people followed Jesus wherever He went. These people saw Him heal sick people, make the blind see, and tenderly hold babies and children. He was a great teacher.

Jesus Christ Dies

Another prophet, Zechariah, wrote that someone would betray the Messiah. (Zechariah 11:12,13; 13:6; Matthew 26:14–16; 27:3–10) This prediction came true, too. Some of the things Jesus said made the religious leaders in Jerusalem mad. One of Jesus' best friends, Judas, led these leaders to Jesus. Judas kissed Jesus on the cheek to show the leaders that He was the Man they should arrest. The leaders took Jesus to court because He said He was God.

The court sentenced Him to die on a cross.

David, a king who lived long ago, described the way the Messiah would die. King David described a crucifixion, but he didn't know anything about crucifixion. David had never seen anyone die that way. (Psalm 22; Matthew 27) Jesus was nailed on a cross on top of a hill called Calvary. He died hours later. Then His body was taken off the cross and put into a tomb. A tomb is a hollowed-out cave where people are buried. A huge stone was rolled in front of the entrance to the tomb so no one could get in or out.

King David also wrote that the Messiah would not stay in the tomb. (Psalm 16:9,10; Acts 2:31) Would you believe that's exactly what happened? This is the biggest miracle of all. On the third day after Jesus died, the stone in front of His tomb was mysteriously rolled away. Jesus came back to life again! All His best friends saw Him. Jesus walked and talked with them and even ate food with them. More than 500 people saw Him alive again!

Jesus' friends are telling everyone about Him. People all over Jerusalem are beginning to believe that Jesus is God. These people are called by a new name—Christians.

I Knew Him! Skit Script

Dan Rathernot: *(Holds the microphone and addresses the crowd.)* Hello. This is Dan Rathernot reporting from Jerusalem. Everyone here is talking about a man named Jesus who is causing excitement. Some say that He is God's Son and others say He's not. But everybody agrees that there's something special about Him. I have found several people who knew Jesus. *(Moves to Zacchaeus. Zacchaeus stands up.)*

Dan Rathernot: The first man I want you to meet is Zacchaeus. He was too short to see Jesus over the heads of the crowd surrounding Jesus, so he climbed a tree to see better. Jesus noticed him and came to his house. Zacchaeus, who do you think Jesus is?

Zacchaeus: He is the Son of God who came to find and save sinners, people who do wrong things. Even though everyone hated me because I was a tax collector, Jesus came to my house. I couldn't believe it! No one ever came to my house, because no one liked me. I cheated people out of their money.

I listened to every word Jesus said. I knew that what I had been doing was wrong, so I gave away half of my money to the poor and paid back all the money I cheated from others. I really love Jesus. He is my Savior and Friend.

Dan Rathernot: Thank you, Zacchaeus. Now I'd like you to meet Martha. *(Moves to Martha's chair. She stands.)* She's a good friend of Jesus. She lives with her brother, Lazarus, and her sister, Mary, in the small town of Bethany. Martha, who do you think Jesus is?

Martha: As soon as I met Jesus, I knew that He is the Christ, the Son of God. But He proved He was God to many people one exciting day. It all happened just after my brother, Lazarus, died. We buried him in a tomb. My sister and I cried and cried.

Four days later, Jesus showed up. I thought it was too late. After all, when you're dead, you're dead. Then Jesus spoke, and Lazarus walked right out of his grave, still wrapped in his grave clothes! Jesus showed that He has power over death when He raised Lazarus from the dead. Only God has power over death. Jesus is truly God.

Dan Rathernot: That's amazing. Thank you Martha. *(Moves to Thomas. Thomas stands.)* This is one of Jesus' twelve disciples. What is your name?

Thomas: Thomas.

Dan Rathernot: What can you tell me about Jesus?

Thomas: I spent three years with Jesus. I watched Him perform many miracles like making blind people see again, healing others who couldn't walk, and calming storms on the Sea of Galilee. But when He died on the cross, I began to doubt He was really the Son of God. After all, why would the Son of God allow Himself to be killed that way? Three days later when my friends told me that Jesus had raised from the dead, I didn't believe it. Then Jesus appeared to me and the other disciples. I even touched the nail wounds in His hands! He really is the Son of God!

Dan Rathernot: *(Moves to Pilate. Pilate stands.)* We are honored to have Pilate, a governor of a country called Rome. He was the man who commanded his soldiers to crucify Jesus. Pilate, what can you tell me about Jesus?

Pilate: I still remember that day like it was yesterday. The religious rulers brought Jesus before me and accused Him of claiming to be the King of the Jews. That was a serious claim. No one could be king except our own ruler, Caesar.

I was impressed by how calm Jesus was. He stood silently while people accused Him of doing bad things. I knew then that Jesus was an innocent man and that His accusers hated Him because they were jealous of Him. I tried to let Him go free, but the angry crowd said no! They wanted a well-known criminal named Barabbas to go free. Although I released Barabbas and sentenced Jesus to die on a cross, I knew what I was doing was wrong. I washed my hands in a bowl of water to show that the innocent blood of Jesus wouldn't be my fault. But somehow, I still feel like I did something terribly wrong.

Dan Rathernot: Thank you, Pilate. *(Moves to Anthony. Anthony stands.)* The last man I want you to hear from is Anthony, one of the Roman soldiers who kept guard over Jesus while He hung on the cross. What can you tell me about Jesus?

Anthony: At first, I didn't believe the story that Jesus was the Son of God. But then things happened that changed my mind. As Jesus hung on the cross with nails through His hands and feet, all of us soldiers were impressed because He still showed love for everyone. The criminals we crucified certainly didn't act that way. They swore and acted badly.

After hanging there in pain for hours, He died. Suddenly, many strange things happened. Tombs were opened and dead people walked around. An earthquake shook everything. The very thick curtain in the temple was torn in half—but no one had touched it. When all these things happened, I realized that we had crucified the Son of God!

Dan Rathernot: Thank you for all these stories about Jesus. You have heard from several people who knew Jesus. Who do you think Jesus is? I hope that these people have helped you make up your mind about whether Jesus was really the Son of God. This is Dan Rathernot from the *Sonshine Jerusalem News*.

Survey:
"Who Do You Say Jesus Is?"

Ask someone, "Who do you say Jesus is? Is He God or is He not God?" Check the answer in the correct box. Then ask the person the reason for his or her answer. Write the answer in the last box.

Person Interviewed	He Is God	He Is Not God	Why Do You Think This?
Mom			
Dad			
Sister			
Brother			
Friend			
Relative			

Powerful Proof

LESSON PLAN

OBJECTIVE: Students will learn that Jesus proved that He was the Son of God through the power of the things He did.

APPLICATION: Students will make a prayer pact in which they record how Jesus powerfully answers their prayers.

LESSON PLAN ELEMENT	ACTIVITY	TIME	SUPPLIES
Opening Activity	*Pleated Power*	7–10	3 glasses; 2 sheets of plain paper; a pitcher of water; paper towels for spills; pictures of a king, a teacher, a doctor, and a weatherman (or other powerful people)
Bible Story—Assorted Scriptures regarding Jesus' power	*Power-Packed Person*	10–15	Bibles; "Power Packed" handouts
Check for Understanding	*I Saw the Power of Jesus*	3–5	"Power Packed" handouts; pencils; colored markers (optional)
Lesson Activity	*Powerful Photographs*	7–10	Bibles; 6 pieces of paper; 6 pencils; construction paper and rolls of toilet paper (optional)
Memory Verse Activity	*Popcorn Power*	3–5	Bible
Application	*My Powerful Friend*	7–10	Slips of paper; pencils
Weekly Assignment	*Powerful Prayer Pacts*	3–5	"My Prayer Pact" handouts; notebooks for journals (optional)

Jesus Christ is the greatest person who ever lived. His moral character, His teachings, and His influence over history demonstrate that He indeed is God. Through two thousand years of advancements in education, technology, philosophy, medicine, and science, mankind has never produced a person who is worthy to be compared with Jesus.

From the beginning of His life, Jesus demonstrated unfailing grace, amazing wisdom, astounding understanding and knowledge, and a power over every force in the universe. His character was pure, selfless, and sinless. The crowds found His compassion constant, and He was humble and meek before His enemies. He treated the poor with respect and children with love and tenderness.

Jesus proved His divine character through His immeasurable love, an unconditional love unique in history. This love was revealed during His life through the many encounters He had with people of all kinds and ages.

Jesus also proved His divine character through the power He displayed over every force on earth. His birth was a powerful event—one that angels announced and wise men came to honor. As a child of twelve, He astounded scholars with the power of His knowledge. As a man, He proved His power over disease by healing many, His power over death by raising Lazarus from the dead, His power over natural forces when He calmed the sea and the wind. He proved His power over temptation and sin when He was tempted by Satan in the wilderness but did not succumb. In every way, His power proved that He is the Son of God.

Elementary children are intrigued by power—perhaps because as children they have so little, either physically or socially. They love to watch television shows or movies about super heroes, and play video games that put themselves in the driver's seat of race cars, fighter jet planes, or submarines. Huge animals like dinosaurs intrigue them.

Children want to know that there is a "force" out there that will wield power in their behalf. In this lesson, the students will learn that Jesus is the only Person who lived on earth who has power over the universe. He used His supernatural power to prove that He is the "sent One" and that He is God.

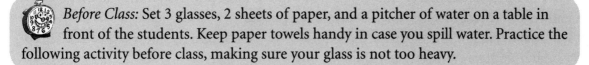

LESSON PLAN

OPENING ACTIVITY: Pleated Power

> *Before Class:* Set 3 glasses, 2 sheets of paper, and a pitcher of water on a table in front of the students. Keep paper towels handy in case you spill water. Practice the following activity before class, making sure your glass is not too heavy.

When students arrive, review the results of the "Who Do You Say Jesus Is?" Survey that the students worked on after the last session. If any of the students encountered a survey respondent who did not believe that Jesus is God, discuss the reasons why that person believed this and why those beliefs are not based on facts.

Today I am going to show you an example of paper power. **Set two of the glasses upside down about six inches apart and put a piece of paper across the glasses to make a bridge.** I have built a paper bridge.

- Do you think this bridge is weak or strong? *(Pretty weak.)*

Pour water into the third glass until it is about half full.

- Do you think my paper bridge will be able to hold up this glass of water? *(No!)*

Demonstrate how the paper isn't able to hold the glass of water. This task seems impossible. But watch as I do something to the sheet of paper to make it more powerful. **Fold the paper into an accordion-style fan. Place it back on the glasses to make a pleated bridge.**

I have pleated my paper to give it more strength or power. Now let's see if our paper bridge will work. **Carefully place the glass on the bridge. As it rests on the bridge say:** Now our bridge is able to hold the glass of water. I made the bridge more powerful by adding the pleats. Power is an important quality. It can help us do things. Let's think about some powerful people in our world.

- What people come to your mind when I mention powerful people? *(Our president; a king; army generals; sports players.)*

Let's think about some of the people in our world today who have power or influence over our world. **Hold up a picture of a king.**

- What makes a king so powerful? *(He has the authority to rule over his kingdom. Whatever he says has to be obeyed.)*

Hold up a picture of a teacher. A teacher has the power to influence us in the things we say or do. A teacher can make a difference in our life. That gives him (her) power, too.

Hold up a picture of a doctor.

- In what ways is a doctor powerful? *(He can help save someone who is dying or sick. He knows how to make people well.)*

The ability to heal gives a doctor power. He knows more about medicines and medical procedures than we do. When we are sick we go to a doctor for help.

Hold up a picture of a weatherman. Some of the most powerful things on earth are weather occurrences such as tornadoes and hurricanes. A weatherman helps us learn about their arrival and gives us warnings to keep safe. We look to him (her) for advice and authority on the weather. Authority is a kind of power.

These people all have power and authority in different ways. But there was a man who lived long ago who had more power and authority than all these people combined. I am talking about Jesus Christ. Even though He came to earth as a Man, He is fully God. In Matthew 28:18, Jesus said, "All authority [or power] in heaven and on earth has been given to Me."

Jesus is a King, and a powerful teacher. He has power over sickness and death. He also has the power to stop a storm in its tracks. Today, we are going to look at the power of Jesus. His power will show us that He is truly the Son of God.

BIBLE STORY: Power-Packed Person

Make sure every student has a Bible. Distribute the "Power Packed" cartoon handouts and pencils.

- If you had special powers like Superman, how would people know about your powers? *(They would see you flying over buildings. They could hear about how you rescued people.)*

To let people know that you have super powers, you would show them what mighty things you could do. You would perform feats of bravery and strength. Superman is a made-up person, but Jesus is very real. Jesus has great power. He proved He was God by doing things that no one else could do. The Bible tells about many of these things. Let's look at six ways Jesus proved He is God through using His power.

Look at the first cartoon on your "Power Packed" sheets.

- What is happening in this picture? *(The angels are telling the shepherds that Jesus is born. The star is over the place where Jesus is born.)*

Each Christmas, people love to tell the story of the birth of Jesus. He was born in a stable in Bethlehem. Angels appeared in the night sky to tell the shepherds that God's only Son had been born. The shepherds ran to see baby Jesus. After they had seen Him, they ran to tell all their friends about the good news that the Messiah was born.

- What do you remember about the Christmas story? *(Allow students to help you retell the story of Jesus' birth. Have them turn to Luke 2:1–20 where the story of Jesus' birth is found.)*

Jesus' birth was a miracle. In Luke 1:35, an angel told Mary, Jesus' mother, that the Spirit of God would be the power that caused Jesus to be born. We can call this the Powerful Birth.

No one else in history has ever been born like that. Write "Powerful Birth" next to the picture of the shepherds hearing about Jesus' birth from the angels.

Direct the students' attention to the second cartoon.

- What is happening in this picture? (*A boy is talking to some men. People are holding a scroll.*)

Have you ever heard the saying, "Knowledge is power"? The more you know, the more you can do. For example, if you know how to operate a computer, you can do so many more things. You can get many kinds of jobs. But if you don't know how to run a computer, you are limited in what you can do.

- In what other ways can you use knowledge to help you? (*If I know a lot, I can do well on tests. I know how to fix my own bike so I don't need to pay for it to be fixed at the bike shop.*)

Jesus had supernatural knowledge-power. In Luke 2:41–52, the Bible tells us about something that happened when Jesus was a twelve-year-old boy. **Point out the verses in your Bible.** Joseph and Mary, Jesus' parents, took Him to the temple one day. A temple was like a church where people learned about God. In the temple, teachers studied the Scriptures. They knew a lot about God's Word. When Jesus came, He began teaching these teachers about God's Word. Everyone was amazed!

- How could a mere boy know so much about the Bible? (*He is God. He knows everything. The Bible is His book.*)

Write "Knowledge Power" next to the second cartoon.

Now we come to an area of power that we don't often think about. Jesus had power over temptation. Temptation is when you feel like doing something wrong, like telling a lie or getting mad, or swearing. All of us are tempted, and all of us sometimes do wrong things when we are tempted.

Jesus was the only Person in history who never did anything wrong. He never disobeyed God, His Father. But that doesn't mean He didn't have temptations. In fact, Jesus was tempted by the devil himself.

Point out the third cartoon.

Just before Jesus began His ministry, He spent forty days in the wilderness praying. He was preparing Himself to do all the things He knew He had to do in the next three years. While He was praying, He didn't eat any solid food. During those forty days, Satan tried to get Jesus to obey his orders. Satan told Jesus to turn the stones into bread. Jesus was very hungry and He had the power to turn stones into bread. But Jesus would never do what Satan tempted Him to do. **Point out Luke 4:12 and say,** Instead, Jesus said, "Do not put the Lord your God to the test." Satan had to leave because he found out that he couldn't make Jesus sin.

- Why does Jesus have power over sin? (*He's God and God can't sin. He's stronger than the devil.*)

Next to the third cartoon, write "Power Over Sin."

- What is happening in the fourth cartoon? *(Jesus is helping someone. Jesus is healing a man.)*

Jesus also had power over disease. He could heal anyone anywhere. The man in this picture has a terrible disease called leprosy. It spread all over his body, and people would not let him come near them. He had to live alone. No one knew how to cure this disease. Luke 5:12–15 tells us that Jesus healed this man completely. **Point out the verses in your Bible.** Healing someone was not hard for Jesus to do. He just reached out His hand, touched the man, and said, "Be clean." The man was healed!

Next to the fourth cartoon, write "Power Over Disease."

Point out the fifth cartoon.

- Do you know a Bible story about the power of Jesus that goes with this picture? *(Jesus made the storm stop.)*

Jesus had power over nature. **Point out Luke 8:22–25. Allow students to help you tell this story.** One day, Jesus and His disciples got in a boat to sail across a big lake. Jesus fell asleep. Meanwhile, a huge storm came up. The disciples thought they were going to drown. They woke up Jesus. When Jesus got up, He told the wind and the waves to be calm and the storm stopped. No one else could do!

- Can you think of any other Bible stories about Jesus that show His power over nature? *(He fed thousands of people with two fish and five loaves of bread. He walked on top of water.)*

Next to the fifth cartoon, write "Power Over Nature."

The last picture shows a power that really amazed people. Jesus proved He had power over death by raising someone from the dead! Jesus raised Lazarus from the dead after Lazarus had been in the grave for four days! That is a long time.

- Can you tell us what happened in the story? *(Allow children to help you tell the following story.)*

Point out the story in John 11:1–44. Lazarus was very sick. He was one of Jesus' best friends. But Jesus waited for two more days after He learned about Lazarus before He went to the town where Lazarus and his two sisters lived. By the time He got there, Lazarus had already been dead for four days. Jesus went to the tomb where Lazarus was buried. All Jesus said was, "Lazarus, come out!" and Lazarus came alive and walked out of the tomb!

Write "Power Over Death" next to the last cartoon.

- Which power is most amazing to you and why? *(Allow students to give responses.)*

CHECK FOR UNDERSTANDING: I Saw the Power of Jesus

Jesus truly is an amazing Person. He proved He is God by the things He did. There was nothing that was too hard for Jesus to do.

BEGINNING THE CHRISTIAN ADVENTURE

Do you see those speech balloons in each of our cartoon pictures? Imagine that you were at that scene when Jesus showed His power. What do you think each person might have said when he or she saw Jesus' power? Write your answer in each of the speech balloons.

Give students a few minutes to write conversation in the speech balloons. Circulate through your group, helping students think of things they could write. Allow students to color their cartoons if you have time and if they enjoy that activity.

LESSON ACTIVITY: Powerful Photographs

Write the following two phrases on the chalkboard:

- Description of our photo

- Why this photo demonstrates Jesus' power as God

Divide your class into six groups. Make sure each group has a Bible. Give each group a piece of paper and pencil. (If you are working with a small group, you can have students demonstrate some of the scenes, then discuss the others.)

Sometimes a photograph can be very powerful. Pictures of a disaster such as a flood can encourage people to send help. A picture taken of a robbery can help put the thief in jail. Today we are going to make "real-life" photos of what we've just learned about Jesus. We learned six different ways Jesus demonstrated that He was the most powerful Person, the Son of God.

In your groups, you will demonstrate one type of power through a still-life photo. To make the still-life photo, your group members will pose for one important scene from the story you will be assigned. Choose one person in your group to describe your scene to the class and tell why it demonstrates Jesus' power. Assign one person to write the story on your piece of paper. Work on the narration as a group using the information on the board to help you. **Assign the following still-life photo scenes and provide descriptions if necessary:**

- Still-Life Photo One—Powerful Birth (Luke 2:1–20) *(Shepherds kneeling before the angels: Students may choose to make shepherd's crooks, wings, halos, etc., out of paper.)*

- Still-Life Photo Two—Knowledge Power (Luke 2:41–52) *(Jesus as a boy standing and teaching before a group of seated men: Students may choose to make a scroll.)*

- Still-Life Photo Three—Power Over Sin (Luke 4:1–13) *(Jesus kneeling in prayer while Satan tempts Him to turn a stone into bread: Students may choose to make a stone and loaf of bread out of paper.)*

- Still-Life Photo Four—Power Over Disease (Luke 5:12–15) *(Jesus in a crowd touching the leper and healing him: Students may choose to wrap strips of paper on parts of leper's body as bandages.)*

- Still-Life Photo Five—Power Over Nature (Luke 8:22–25) *(Jesus standing up in a boat with His disciples seated. Jesus' hand is raised to calm the sea: Students can make a boat out of chairs or a table, and add paper waves.)*

- Still-Life Photo Six—Power Over Death (John 11:1–44) *(Lazarus walking out of the tomb with Jesus and crowd watching: Students may wrap Lazarus in toilet paper if they choose.)*

Give students five minutes to work on these still-life photos and narration. Circulate among groups to make sure both parts are being done. The narration is very important, and students tend to forget to work on it. After five minutes, call the students together, and allow them to present their still-life photos to the class.

After each presentation, summarize how Jesus demonstrated power. Conclude with this:

Jesus was truly the Son of God. Only the Son of God would have such a powerful and miraculous birth and have that much knowledge as a young boy. Only the Son of God could have power over disease, nature, sin, and death.

 Teaching Tip: A fun option would be to snap a photo of each presentation and put it on your bulletin board!

MEMORY VERSE ACTIVITY: Popcorn Power

Matthew 28:18—"Then Jesus came to them and said, 'All authority in heaven and on earth has been given to Me.'"

We have learned a lot about power. People like police officers and judges have power called authority. This means that they have a right to affect people's lives. For example, a police officer can arrest someone who is committing a crime and take that person to jail. A judge can sentence a criminal to many years in jail.

Jesus also has authority. Earlier, we read how He claims to have all authority, including authority over heaven and earth. Let's read this verse again. **Read Matthew 28:18.**

Have you ever watched popcorn pop? It has power like a mini-explosion. Yet its power results in something good to eat. To help us remember that Jesus has good power, let's act like popcorn popping.

Have students sit in a circle, fanning out to give each other room to move. Assign each person a word of the memory verse. If you have a large group, make two circles. If you have a smaller group, assign more than one word to a person.

When you say "go," students will say their words in order by "popping" up when it is their turn. After "popping" through the verse several times, calmly say the verse as a group several times. Then allow volunteers to try saying the verse from memory.

APPLICATION: My Powerful Friend

Jesus wants to be our best friend. Remember our paper bridge? We are like the weak bridge I made out of paper. We have trouble living the way God wants us to live. Instead, we do wrong things and don't think about God. But Jesus wants to use His power to help us live for Him. His power makes us strong like the pleated bridge.

Now that we have learned about the power of Jesus, let's think about how His power can help us. Let's look at three areas.

1. Power to trust God

2. Power over temptation

3. Prayer power

Go through each of these areas, discussing how the power of Jesus can help kids in everyday life. Write your ideas on a chalkboard. The following are some suggestions in each area:

1. Power to trust God

   (Because I know Jesus has power over everything, I can ask Him to help me stop being afraid of the dark, of lightning, of being alone, of what others may say about me.)

   (Because Jesus has all power, I can trust His Word, the Bible, to guide my life.)

2. Power over temptation

   (Because Jesus has power over sin, I can ask Him to help me do what is right when I am tempted to lie, cheat on a test, get angry with my sister or brother.)

   (I can ask Jesus to help me say no to drugs.)

3. Prayer power

   (Because Jesus is all-powerful, I can pray, asking Him to help me study for a test, obey my parents, remember to clean my room, or be kind to my friends.)

   (As I pray, Jesus will use His power to help me be more like Him.)

Once you have made your list on the board, ask each person in your class to silently pick one idea that he or she needs help with this week. Pass out slips of paper and pencils. Have students write down their idea, then fold up the piece of paper so no one else sees it. Encourage students to follow through with their idea this week.

Pray, asking God to help students trust the power of Jesus to live godly lives. Invite volunteers to pray aloud after you pray. Then close by thanking Jesus for being such a powerful friend.

WEEKLY ASSIGNMENT: Powerful Prayer Pacts

Teaching Tip: You may want to purchase small notebooks for your students to use as prayer journals. If you do, invite students to share what they wrote in the prayer journals each week during the rest of the sessions.

Let's imagine you are the son or daughter of a very powerful king. You love him very much.

He gives you anything you need and everything you want that is good for you. You don't live in the castle with your father, the king, but in a house some distance from him. But you can talk to him anytime by phone. He will always take time to talk to you. How often will you call? I'm sure we would all call at least once a day or many times a day just to talk to him and get his advice.

This is a picture of our relationship with Jesus Christ. He is the King of kings, and we learned today that He is very powerful.

- How do we keep in touch with Him? *(Through prayer.)*

- How often can we pray? *(Anytime we want.)*

Prayer gives us power because it connects us with Jesus, our power source. With His power, we become strong like our pleated bridge. This week, let's make a powerful prayer pact. Let's agree to bring things to Jesus in prayer every day. Let's see what will happen when we do. **Hand out copies of "My Prayer Pact." You may want to have students put their copies in a notebook or journal. Make available a new Prayer Pact each week.**

Every day, record the things you pray about. At the end of the week, record how Jesus answered your prayers and the times you felt His power. Then bring this prayer pact to our next session so we can discuss His power.

My Prayer Pact

Things I prayed about

Sunday:

Monday:

Tuesday:

Wednesday:

Thursday:

Friday:

Saturday:

Ways Jesus answered my prayers and how I felt His power through prayer:

Power-Packed

① _____ _____

② _____ _____

Power-Packed

③ _____
_____

④ _____
_____

Power-Packed

_____

_____

_____

_____

Resurrection Power

LESSON PLAN

OBJECTIVE: Students will learn that Jesus died on the cross to pay for the sins they have committed.

APPLICATION: Students will be challenged to become members of God's family or to share their faith with others.

LESSON PLAN ELEMENT	ACTIVITY	TIME	SUPPLIES
Opening Activity	*"Eggs"actly Right*	7–10	"Resurrection Eggs®" (see Resources to order), or 1 dozen large plastic eggs and pictures or small items to go inside of eggs (see directions below); timer
Bible Story—Assorted Scriptures about the resurrection	*The Resurrection*	10–15	Bible; "Resurrection Eggs"
Lesson Activity	*Would You Like to Belong to God's Family?*	7–10	A copy of *Would You Like to Belong to God's Family?* for each student (see Resources to order) or other children's gospel tract
Check for Understanding	*It's for Sure*	7–10	
Application	*Share in a Pair*	3–5	*Would You Like to Belong to God's Family?* booklets
Memory Verse Activity	*Crack an Egg*	3–5	Basket; plastic eggs; slips of paper
Weekly Assignment	*Getting Out the News*	3–5	*Would You Like to Belong to God's Family?* booklets

Jesus' crucifixion demoralized His followers; the terror-stricken little band scattered. Jesus' enemies were celebrating their victory. But three days after the crucifixion, a miracle occurred: Jesus rose from the dead.

Within a few weeks, His once cowardly followers were fearlessly proclaiming His resurrection, a fact that changed the course of history. Followers of Jesus Christ were not people who promoted an ethical code of a dead founder, but rather those who had had vital contact with a living Lord. Jesus Christ still lives today, and He is anxiously waiting to work in the lives of those who trust Him. He is vitally interested in the lives of the elementary students who come into your classroom each week.

The new life and courage demonstrated by the early Christians is vividly described by J. B. Phillips in the Preface to his *Letters to Young Churches:*

> The great difference between present-day Christianity and that of which we read in these letters is that to us it is primarily a performance; to them it was a real experience. We are apt to reduce the Christian religion to a code, or at best a rule of heart and life. To these men it is quite plainly the invasion of their lives by a new quality of life altogether. They do not hesitate to describe this as Christ "living in" them.

> Mere moral reformation will hardly explain the transformation and the exuberant vitality of these men's lives—even if we could prove a motive for such reformation, and certainly the world around offered little encouragement to the early Christian! We are practically driven to accept their own explanation, which is that their little human lives had, through Christ, been linked up with the very life of God.

> Many Christians today talk about the "difficulties of our times" as though we have to wait for better ones before the Christian religion can take root. These pessimists are especially downcast about the upcoming generation of young people. But this is not a godly attitude. It is heartening to remember that the faith of the first followers of Christ took root and flourished in conditions that would have killed anything less vital in a matter of weeks.

> These early Christians were on fire with the conviction that they had become, through Christ, literal sons of God; they were pioneers of a new humanity, founders of a new kingdom.

Your young students can also catch this fire for our Lord. Their minds are receptive; many are looking for answers that they already understand the world does not offer.

As you prepare for this lesson, pray for each student individually. The material presents the gospel in a clear manner and also shows children who are already believers how to share their faith. Determine where each one of your students stands in relation to God's kingdom. Then ask God to open the hearts of those who do not yet know Him as Savior and Lord.

LESSON PLAN

OPENING ACTIVITY: "Eggs"actly Right

The opening activity and Bible story are based on a product called "Resurrection Eggs®" produced by FamilyLife of Little Rock, Arkansas. Although the lesson is complete without using the "Resurrection Eggs," they will enhance your story presentation and serve as a valuable hands-on activity in many other settings, including Easter. The package includes a carton of one dozen colored plastic eggs that contain items to help your students comprehend the Easter story. The accompanying booklet provides a clear lesson on how to use the eggs when telling the story and suggests how to use the eggs in different ways. To order "Resurrection Eggs," see the Resources at the back of this book.

> *Before Class:* If you are assembling your own egg visuals, purchase a dozen colored, plastic eggs. If possible, select all different colors. Also obtain an egg carton. Place the following small items into each egg. You may use either the actual items or pictures of them.
>
> 1. Fringed leaf to represent a palm branch
> 2. Silver coins such as quarters or "play" coins
> 3. Praying hands
> 4. Narrow leather strip (e.g., piece of leather shoe lace)
> 5. Twig with thorns (e.g., rose branch)
> 6. Wooden cross
> 7. Nails
> 8. Die
> 9. Piece of white cloth
> 10. Perfumed cotton ball
> 11. Stone
> 12. Nothing
>
> Use a permanent marker to mark the item number (1 through 12) on the outside of the eggshell. Be sure to leave Egg 12 empty. Also number the egg depressions inside the egg carton with numbers 1 through 12. Set the egg carton in a central location. Hide the eggs around the room.

When students arrive, discuss the answers to prayer that they recorded in their Prayer Pacts. Hand out a new sheet and encourage them to use it during the next week. Then form two groups. Assign numbers 1 through 12 to group members. If you have fewer than 12 students in a group, assign some students more than one number.

> *Teaching Tip:* Hide two sets of "Resurrection Eggs" and have groups hunt for eggs at the same time.

Today we are going to have an "Eggs"actly Right Egg Hunt. Let's see how quickly we can locate the twelve eggs I have hidden around the room.

This is a relay race. Each egg has a number on it that corresponds to the number of one person in your group. For example, the person who was assigned #1 will hunt for Egg 1 and bring it back to the carton and put it into hole number 1. That person is not allowed to move an egg with any other number on it, so he may find several eggs before he finds the right one. DO NOT open any of the eggs.

As soon as Egg 1 is safely in its place in the egg carton, the person with #2 can hunt for Egg 2. The game will continue until the last egg is put into the egg carton. Let's see which group can find the eggs in the shortest amount of time.

When hunting for eggs, you are not allowed to run, only walk. If you run, you will have to return to the egg carton and start over. The other people in your group can cheer you on and call out places to look. **Select one group to go first. These students will leave the room while the other group hides the eggs. When the first group returns, say:** Group 1, are you ready? Go!

Time the game to see how long Group 1 takes. Then have Group 2 leave the room while Group 1 hides the eggs. Time Group 2's effort to find the eggs. Applaud the winning group! Then have students sit in a circle.

In this game, you had to find the eggs in exactly the right order. Doing anything exactly right is difficult. People often make mistakes, forget how to do something, or just get mixed up. Sometimes people get frustrated or angry and quit what they are doing.

- What is something you did this past week that you needed to get exactly right but you messed up on it? *(My science experiment. Making a cake. Jumping off a ramp with my bike.)*

- How did not getting it right make you feel? *(Mad; sad; like I failed.)*

- What's something hard you have to do that you feel you can never get right? *(Math story problems. Dribbling a basketball while running down the court. Practicing piano lessons.)*

There is only one Person who has lived on this earth who has done everything exactly right. By now, I'm sure you know that this Person is Jesus.

Jesus was born at exactly the right time—just as the Old Testament prophets predicted. He grew up to be a Man just as God expected and wanted. Jesus didn't commit a single sin. He treated people right. He did everything in His life exactly right at exactly the right time.

Now imagine that you are one of Jesus' close friends. You know that He does everything right because you have been with Him and have watched Him for years. You have great hopes for what Jesus will do in the future. It seems like everything is going just right.

Then things begin to happen that you don't like. Very bad things. In fact, everything seems to be falling apart. Nothing seems right anymore. Jesus is taken away by soldiers. A horrible trial is underway. It looks like the government plans to kill Him. You begin to wonder if Jesus is really the Son of God because He doesn't seem to be able to control the situation. If He is God, then how can He let these terrible things happen?

What did happen to Jesus? The story we will hear today is the most famous and important true event in history!

BIBLE STORY: The Resurrection

If you are using the "Resurrection Eggs" for your Bible story, follow the lesson plan in the "Resurrection Eggs" booklet. Skip the following Bible story and resume this lesson with the questions following the story.

If you are using eggs you assembled yourself, you can tell this story in two ways, depending on how familiar your students are with the resurrection story.

1. Hand out the eggs. Have each student open his egg in the appropriate order and tell what the item represents and how it fits into the story of Jesus' death and resurrection. Read the Scripture passage that goes along with that item and elaborate on that part of the story.

2. Use the eggs to tell the story yourself. Open each egg in order, read the Scripture passage, and tell that part of the story. When finished, hand out the eggs to your students and have them retell the story to you.

Before Class: Carefully read all four accounts of the death and resurrection of Jesus: Matthew 26–28; Mark 14–16; Luke 22–24; and John 18–20. Jot down points you want to emphasize.

At the beginning of your story time, point out the four places in the Gospels that describe the death and resurrection of Jesus. Explain that this story is so important that God included it in all these places in the Bible. As you tell the story, include the facts that you jotted down.

EGG NO.	ITEM IN EGG	SCRIPTURE PASSAGE	PART OF STORY IT REPRESENTS
1	Palm leaf	Matthew 21:1–9	During the triumphal entry of Jesus into Jerusalem, the people cheered Him and waved palm branches.
2	Coins	Matthew 26:14–16	Judas was paid thirty pieces of silver by the religious leaders to tell them where Jesus was so they could arrest Him in private.
3	Praying hands	Matthew 26:36–39	Jesus prayed in the Garden of Gethsemane because He knew how hard the suffering He would endure would be.
4	Leather strip	Matthew 27:11–14, 24–26	The soldiers arrested Jesus, brought Him to court, and whipped Him.
5	Thorn branch	Matthew 26:27–31	The soldiers put a crown of thorns on Jesus' head to make fun of Him as King of kings.
6	Cross	Matthew 27:32,33	Jesus carried His cross to the hill called Golgotha.

Egg No.	Item in Egg	Scripture Passage	Part of Story It Represents
7	Nails	John 19:17,18	The soldiers nailed spikes into Jesus' hands and feet.
8	Die	John 19:23,24	The soldiers took Jesus' clothes and gambled to see who would get them.
9	White cloth	Matthew 27:57–61	After Jesus died, two of His friends wrapped His body in white linen cloth and laid Him in a tomb.
10	Perfumed cotton ball	Luke 23:55–24:1	The women went to the tomb to put spices and perfume on Jesus' body.
11	Stone	Luke 24:2	The women found that the huge stone had been rolled away.
12	Empty	Luke 24:3–8	The tomb was empty! Jesus had risen from the dead!

- What is the most important part of the story to you? (*That Jesus died for my sins. That Jesus rose from the dead like He said He would.*)

- How does it make you feel knowing that Jesus had to pay for the wrong things you have done? (*I feel very sad. Sorry that I did those wrong things.*)

Knowing about Jesus' death on the cross and His resurrection is the most important fact you will ever learn in your lifetime. That's because His death allows us to become part of God's family and live with Him forever. Right now, let's learn about what God will do for us because of what Jesus did on the cross.

Lesson Activity: Would You Like to Belong to God's Family?

During this activity, you will be reading through a gospel tract with your students. The booklet *Would You Like to Belong to God's Family?* is a children's version of the *Four Spiritual Laws,* one of the most effective gospel tracts available.

In your class, you will probably have a few children who have had a lot of spiritual training from godly parents and other children who either do not know Christ as their Savior or have not received much spiritual training. The students who have heard the gospel message may become bored and cause distractions. Therefore, this activity has a dual purpose. The more spiritually mature children will learn how to share the tract with a friend or relative. The others will receive a clear gospel presentation.

To accomplish these purposes, ask another adult to help you in this activity. Divide your students into two groups: those you are sure are believers and those you're unsure of or who are not believers. Give each student a copy of the booklet. Have your helper go through the booklet with the children who are believers, showing them how to read

through it with a friend. Remember that even though children from godly homes may seem like believers, occasionally a child will realize that he still needs to take the step of salvation. Also advise the children who are learning to share their faith that if their friend receives Christ as Savior through the booklet, they need to tell a Christian adult.

You take the other group, and read through the booklet with them. Ask for a response to the prayer of salvation. If you have several who indicate that they want to receive Christ, ask your helper to take a few of them and go through the rest of the booklet so that these children get as much individual attention as possible.

The following are some tips for sharing the gospel with children.

- Show the child you love and care for him. This may be the only opportunity he has ever had to discuss personal spiritual issues with an adult.

- Listen carefully to what the child has to say. That will give you an indication of where he is in his spiritual journey. And he will be able to express what he does not understand to you.

- When you come to the part in the booklet that asks the child for a decision about believing in Christ, be sensitive to God's timing. Some children will feel very bad about their sins. Others will simply want to love God and have Him love them. Still others will not be ready to make a commitment to Christ. Do not force decisions because children will often do what adults say even when they disagree.

- Rejoice with the child who commits his life to Christ. This is a momentous decision and your reaction will help this new believer rejoice too.

- Help each child to acquire his own Bible to read.

CHECK FOR UNDERSTANDING: It's for Sure!

After reading through the booklet, talk to each student individually to make sure he or she understands the plan of salvation. When you talk to each student individually, ask these questions:

1. How does a person get to heaven?

2. Have you ever made the decision to receive Christ as your Savior?

If the student gives wrong answers or seems confused, review pages 10–13 in *Would You Like to Belong to God's Family?* Remember, only God knows for sure the condition of each person's heart, but we can consider a person's answers and the fruit in his or her life to help us gauge where that person is in his or her spiritual journey.

Keep a record of the answers you receive to help you determine how to relate to each student in your class. As you continue in this series, your notes will help you pray for that child and gear your lessons toward his or her spiritual maturity.

APPLICATION: Share in a Pair

You have had a chance to hear me present the booklet *Would You Like to Belong to God's Family?* Now is your chance to practice sharing that good news with someone else. Find a partner and practice reading through the booklet with each other. I will come around to give you tips on how to do your presentation.

Give students a chance to get started, then go around giving tips on how to present the booklet to others. Use the tips given previously in the lesson activity. When everyone has finished, say: Using this small tool will help you tell your friends and family the most important news that they will ever receive! You all did a very good job presenting it to your partners.

MEMORY VERSE ACTIVITY: Crack an Egg

1 Corinthians 15:3,4—"Christ died for our sins, just as the Scriptures said. / He was buried, / and He was raised from the dead on the third day, as the Scriptures said" (NLT).

Before Class: Write one-third of the verse on a slip of paper. Divide sections as indicated. Make twelve slips or four complete verses. (You can divide the verse into two sections if you have a smaller group.) Remove the items from the eggs that were used in the story and set them aside in a safe place. Fill each egg with a slip of paper containing a portion of the verse.

Put the eggs in a basket and hand them out. Instruct students not to open them. Read 1 Corinthians 15:3,4 and say: These verses give us the order of events that took place more than 2,000 years ago. They tell us of the gift of eternal life. Each egg I have passed out contains one-third of this verse. When I say, "Crack an egg," open your egg and look for two other people who can complete the verse with their eggs. Then line up in order and sit down on the floor. The first trio to be seated will read the verse for us. You may need to select another egg from the basket if you cannot find a partner! **(If you have an uneven number of students to play the game, play it more than once so that all students are able to be part of a completed group.)**

When groups are ready, say, "Crack an egg" and let them complete the exercise. Have group members put the verse in order and recite it to each other. Collect the eggs and hand them out again, repeating this activity several times. Then ask for volunteers to repeat the verse from memory.

WEEKLY ASSIGNMENT: Getting Out the News!

Make sure students have their copies of the *Would You Like to Belong to God's Family?* booklet to take home with them.

You have had a chance to practice sharing these four facts with someone in your classroom. This week your assignment is to share the booklet with someone you know, such as a friend or family member. It can be a child or an adult. If possible, pick someone who has not heard about God's free gift of salvation. Remember to ask God to help you before you do this. That is the most important step.

Come back next time ready to share your experiences and feelings before, during, and after your sharing time. Let us know if someone decided to become a member of God's family.

Gracious Savior

LESSON PLAN

OBJECTIVE: Students will recognize Christ's power to overcome problems in their lives.

APPLICATION: Students will examine their lives to commit problem areas to Christ's control.

LESSON PLAN ELEMENT	ACTIVITY	TIME	SUPPLIES
Opening Activity	*The Visitor*	7–10	Items to decorate your room for a visitor. See activity for suggestions.
Bible Story—Acts 7–14, Paul's experience on the road to Damascus	*What a Change!*	10–15	Bibles; "What a Change!" handouts; pencils
Lesson Activity	*Be My Guest*	7–10	Snack with disposable plates, glasses, and napkins; 1 piece of white, unlined paper; black marker
Application	*It's Under Your Control*	7–10	"C'mon In!" handouts; pencils
Check for Understanding	*From Paul to Me*	3–5	"What a Change!" handouts
Memory Verse Activity	*Open Doors*	4–7	2 paper plates; 2 cups; 2 placards; marker; two 18-inch pieces of string
Weekly Assignment	*Change of Heart*	2–3	"C'mon In!" handouts; small heart stickers; stapler

When a person invites Jesus Christ to come into his heart and life to be Savior and Lord, confessing his sin and need of forgiveness, Jesus answers that prayer. He enters the new believer's heart and life.

One reason Jesus comes to live in us is so He can empower us to live godly lives. The Christian life is more than difficult; it is humanly impossible to live. Only Jesus Christ can live it through you as He dwells within you. He wants to think with your mind, express Himself through your emotions, and speak through your voice.

But believers often find themselves filled with many areas of activity—studies, social life, home life—which are out of control. Sinful attitudes and emotions thwart their efforts to do things the godly way. Even elementary students recognize the problem areas in their lives if they will stop to think for a few moments. The reason for out-of-control areas is that we try to handle them by ourselves instead of allowing Jesus Christ to control them.

Each of us has a throne or control center in our lives. Until Jesus Christ comes into our life, our self, or ego, is on the throne. But when Jesus comes in, He wants to assume His place of authority on this throne. We must step down and relinquish the authority of our lives to Him. When Christ controls our lives, we experience purpose and harmony.

Thus the Christian life is more than trying to imitate Christ. It is Christ imparting His life to and living His life through the believer. The Christian life is not what you do for God; it is what He does for and through you. The Christ-controlled life always produces the fruit of the Spirit as listed in Galatians 5:22,23.

Most elementary-age students are seeking something or someone to help them in the areas they cannot manage. Setting more rules or instituting harsher discipline only works on outward behavior. These boys and girls need to learn how to change from the inside— through the power of Jesus Christ.

This lesson emphasizes the importance of Christ living in the believer. The most important part of the study is helping your students invite Christ to control every part of their lives. As you teach this material, cultivate an atmosphere of excitement and awe about the fact that God has chosen to live among and in us.

LESSON PLAN

OPENING ACTIVITY: The Visitor

> *Before Class:* For this activity, invite a guest to your classroom. This person could be the parent of one of your students, a children's pastor, or an adult from your church whom your students know. Give your guest a brief summary of the lesson and what you expect him or her to do. Ask that person to arrive ten minutes after your class time begins, and to take notes on the Bible story and on what he or she likes about your classroom activities. Bring items to decorate the classroom (see directions below).

When your students arrive, announce that a visitor will be coming to your class in a few minutes. Create an atmosphere of excitement by telling students that your visitor will be taking notes during your Bible story time and that you will be treating him or her to a snack after the Bible story. Help students decorate your room to make it special for the guest. The following are some things you could do to decorate your room:

- Hang up crepe paper streamers and balloons in wild colors.

- Build a simple centerpiece for your table out of Legos. Have the centerpiece resemble something that interests your guest such as a car, boat, or building.

- Set a table with disposable plates, glasses, and napkins. Plan to seat your guest at the head of the table. Make that place special by putting a flower beside it, decorating the back of the chair with streamers, or something else to make your guest feel special.

- Make placecards for each person who will sit at the table and share the snack in the Lesson Activity.

- Make a huge group welcome card for the guest from bulletin board paper. Have each student sign it and hang it on the wall. Present it to the visitor at the end of class.

  When you finish decorating, sit in a circle and discuss the following questions.

- What do you like most about having someone special come to visit? (*We get to decorate. Everything seems more fun and special.*)

- Do you know of a person you invited into your home who's even more special than the guest who's coming today? (*Jesus.*)

- What would you do differently if Jesus came in person to your house tonight? (*I'd clean my room. I'd tell all my friends to come over to meet Him.*)

In our time together today, we're going to think about what it means to invite Jesus into our lives. A person does this when he or she asks Him to be Savior.

- Who can tell me from our last lesson what that means? (*Allow for individual responses. Give a brief review of how to become a Christian.*)

- What happened when you shared your *Would You Like to Belong to God's Family?* booklet with someone last week? *(Allow volunteers to share their experiences.)*

If you have asked Jesus to forgive your sins, how does having Him in your life change it? What does He want to do in your life? How should we treat Jesus now that He's our special friend? We will answer all these questions in the rest of our lesson.

Right now, let's look at the life of one man who changed dramatically when he met Jesus face-to-face.

Whenever the guest arrives, stop what you're doing in class and welcome the guest.

BIBLE STORY: What a Change!
Hand out the copies of "What a Change!" Make sure students have pencils.

Almost all the men who wrote the books of the New Testament were disciples of Jesus. They learned from Him for three years while He did His ministry. Then the disciples saw the soldiers crucify Jesus. The disciples also saw Jesus after He was raised from the dead.

One person who wrote at least twelve books of the New Testament was not a disciple of Jesus. This was the apostle Paul. He didn't even become a believer until some time after the resurrection of Jesus. But when he met Jesus, his life turned around.

As I tell this story, listen for ways that the apostle Paul changed when he met Jesus. Think of how his attitudes changed, and write these changes in the first two columns on your worksheet.

The Bible story uses facts from several New Testament passages. Turn to them as you tell the following story. The underlined words are changes that happened in Paul's life. Make sure you emphasize these as you tell the story. Pause in your storytelling to allow students to record their thoughts.

After Jesus went to heaven to be with His Father, the new believers He left behind began to spread the Good News that Jesus is alive. One of these believers was named Stephen. When he told the religious leaders of that day that they were full of sin and needed to repent, the leaders became very angry. They believed that Jesus was only a man, not God's Son. They hated anyone who believed in Jesus.

First, the religious leader spread lies about Stephen. He kept on preaching. When they heard him preaching, they got so angry that they stoned him to death by throwing large rocks at him. There was one young man who was watching all this happen. **Read Acts 7:59–8:1.**

Saul, who later changed his name to Paul, hated the Christians. **Read Acts 8:3,4.**

Saul wanted to destroy every Christian he could. **Read Acts 9:1.** He was so intent on hurting Jesus' followers that he went to the high priest in Jerusalem and asked for official letters allowing him to arrest all the Christians in the city of Damascus. **Read Acts 9:2.**

Have you ever seen a person who is so filled with hate that it takes over his or her whole life? That's the way Saul was. <u>All he could think about was stopping this new religion about Jesus.</u> The Christians were very afraid of Saul.

Saul could hardly wait to get to Damascus. Many of the believers he wanted to arrest in Jerusalem had run to that city to get away. But they weren't going to get away from Saul! He and several other people took off for Damascus right away.

Something amazing happened to Saul when he got close to Damascus. **Read Acts 9:3–9.** This was the moment Saul believed in Jesus. His life was never the same again. <u>All the hatred he had was gone!</u>

The Lord spoke to a believer named Ananias and asked him to do a very scary thing. Ananias obeyed God even though he was afraid. **Read Acts 9:10–18.**

Saul was so changed that his behavior amazed everyone. <u>He began telling everyone about Jesus.</u> **Read Acts 9:19–22.**

The same religious leaders who had killed Stephen for preaching about Jesus now began plotting to kill Saul. <u>But Saul did not stop telling others about Jesus.</u> **Read Acts 9:23–28.**

Soon after he became a Christian, <u>Saul changed his name to Paul.</u> <u>He went to many places helping other people.</u> **Read Acts 14:21–23.** <u>Paul also spent a lot of time praying.</u> **Read Acts 13:1–3.**

What amazing changes we see in Paul's life! He gives all the credit to Jesus living in him and helping him think and do what is right. He describes his new life like this: **Read Romans 8:9,10.** Now he loved people instead of hating them. He helped them instead of hurting them. Paul refers to his new way of living as Christ living in us.

- Why do you think meeting Jesus on the road to Damascus was so shocking to Paul? (*He didn't believe Jesus was alive. He'd been trying to kill Jesus' followers.*)

- Why do you think all the other believers were so afraid of Paul at first? (*They thought he was just pretending to be a Christian. They thought he still wanted to kill them.*)

- How do you think these believers felt after they saw how Jesus had changed Paul's heart and attitudes? (*They were probably very excited. They thanked God.*)

When a person asks Jesus to forgive his sins, the Holy Spirit comes to live in his life. Good changes start to happen. Soon, even other people notice these good changes.

Allow volunteers to read what they wrote on their "What a Change!" sheets about the apostle Paul. Encourage other students to write down new ideas.

In our next activity, we will discover what it means to have Jesus living in us through His Holy Spirit.

LESSON ACTIVITY: Be My Guest

Before Class: Arrange a snack that your students can serve to your guest. You could have bite-size pieces of fruit, crackers, and water, or cookies, pretzels, and chocolate milk.

Assign your students to do the following:

- One or more students to converse with the guest while you bring out the food after the Bible story.

- One student to escort your guest to his or her place at the head of the table.

- Several students to serve the food and drink to your guest.

- Several students as a clean-up crew for when the snack time is over.

When arrangements are all done, turn your students' attention to your guest. Tell them a little about your guest or have your guest tell a little about himself or herself. Then say:

We have prepared a little snack in your honor. **Have the assigned student guide the guest to his or her place at the table. Have students sit down. Ask your guest to thank God for the food. Then enjoy your snack, encouraging conversation around the table.**

While your students are finishing their snack, say: It's fun to have someone special come to eat with us. We're so glad our guest could visit us.

Just like I invited a guest to our classroom this morning, when we became one of God's children, we invited Jesus to come and live in our life.

Here's the promise Jesus gives us about this: **Read Revelation 3:20.** The door in this verse is the door to your life. Jesus wants to come in and eat with you. When the Bible says that Jesus wants to sit down and eat with you, this means something special. The important part of sitting at someone's table is not the food, but getting to know each other. It means welcoming that person into every part of your home. We call this *fellowship*.

Once Jesus comes into your life, He will never leave you. He also comes to help you. He promises this in the Bible. **Read Hebrews 13:5b–6.**

When our class time is over, our guest will leave. But Jesus is more than a guest. When we became a part of God's family, He became like a big brother to us. We get to talk to Him in prayer; He comes to live inside us through His Holy Spirit.

But what happens when you sin? Does Jesus leave then? No. But when we sin, it's like doing something bad to our brother or sister. We know we've done something wrong, so we don't talk to that person. We don't like being with them because we feel guilty. Our fellowship is broken, but we are still part of the family.

If you held up a sparkling white sheet, everyone would see how clean and bright it is. **Hold up a white piece of paper.** But if you put a small blot of dirt in the middle of that sheet, what would people notice about the sheet? They wouldn't notice how clean and bright most of the sheet is. **Put a large black dot on the paper.** They'd notice that one dirty spot. That's how sin stains our life. When we sin, that dirty spot messes up our life.

Sin is not pleasing to God. He can't have fellowship with us as long as we are sinning. His Spirit lets us know that what we are doing is wrong. That's why we feel guilty about our sin.

But we can restore our fellowship with God. To do that, we must confess or admit our sin to Him. He takes the dirty spot off our life and makes it clean again. **Read 1 John 1:9.** When we sincerely confess our sin, God restores our fellowship with Him. We can go back to talking with Him all the time.

APPLICATION: It's Under Your Control

Pass out the "C'mon In!" handouts and pencils. It's important to invite Jesus to be the head of everything in your life. But sometimes we have a hard time letting Him control certain things. Let me give you an example.

Jason has a video-game machine. He loves playing video games on it. He spends every minute he can playing video games, so he often doesn't get his homework done. Sometimes he doesn't do the chores his mother asked him to do. He knows that his video-game playing is out of control, but he doesn't know how to stop playing so much.

Jason has a problem. He has never asked Jesus to take charge of how he uses his time. He needs to ask Jesus to control this part of his life. It's not wrong to play video games. But it is wrong to let playing video games run your life.

All of us have things in our lives that we haven't given over to Jesus to control. What do you have in your life that you have not given over to Jesus? Perhaps it's the kind of television shows you watch. Maybe these shows have bad scenes in them or the actors use bad language. Or you might have something you own that means so much to you that it has become the most important thing in your life. This may be a bike or even money.

- What is one thing in your life that you treasure above everything else you own? (*My bike; my video games; a computer.*)

- What do you spend the most time doing in your free time? (*Watching TV; playing baseball; reading mystery books.*)

On your sheet you will see a blueprint of a house with several rooms. In your house plan, draw three or four things that you spend a lot of time doing (not counting sleeping or doing homework) or that mean a lot to you. They aren't necessarily bad things—unless they control your time or attitudes. Are these things more important to you than Jesus? As an example, a television has already been drawn for you in the family room. For many of us, television can be a problem. Draw each thing in the room where you use it. You might even draw something in your closet.

Give students a few minutes to draw. Some may have a hard time thinking of what to

include. **Help them with suggestions about things they spend too much time doing or things that they consider their most important possessions.**

Jesus wants to direct each part of our life so that we can do what's right and so we can have joy and peace. Now that we have thought about the most important things in our lives, let's give them over to Jesus to control. I will pray a prayer that asks Jesus to take control of everything. Think of Him going into each room on your blueprint and taking charge of what you have drawn in that room. Pray along with me silently. When I finish praying, I will pause for a few minutes. When I do, silently talk to God. One by one, name each of the things you drew in your house. Tell Jesus that you are giving Him control of each thing. **Pray the following prayer:**

Dear Jesus, I need You. There are things in my life that have been out of control. I know that this is a sin. I thank You for forgiving my sins when You died on the cross for me. I now invite you to control everything in my life. I want everything I do to be pleasing to You. Thank You for caring so much for me that You want to help me with everything I do, think, and say. Amen.

I am now going to pause to give you time to silently talk to Jesus about the things you drew in your house. When you finish praying silently, sit quietly until the other kids finish their prayers.

Pause to let students pray. When all have finished, say, As you go through this week, you will probably find yourself taking control of these areas again. Old habits are hard to break. When you do, pray right away, asking Jesus to take control instead. You may have to pray this prayer many times. But Jesus, with His power and His love for you, will help you control all these things in your life.

If you ask Jesus to help you as soon as you see yourself messing up again, He will help you right away. Then your life will begin to change. Like the apostle Paul, your attitudes and actions will change.

CHECK FOR UNDERSTANDING: From Paul to Me

Let's think about what we've done during this lesson. We treated our guest to a snack and learned that we also invited Jesus into our life when we became a child of God. He wants to live His life in you. Then we prayed a prayer to invite Jesus to control everything in our life.

Let's name some ways our life will change. Look back at the chart you filled out about the apostle Paul. What things in that chart do you think will happen in your life when you let Jesus control everything?

Help students apply the changes they noted about Paul's life to their own and write it in the third column. Discuss how only Jesus can make true changes for good in our lives.

MEMORY VERSE ACTIVITY: Open Doors

Revelation 3:20—"Here I am! I stand at the door and knock. If anyone hears my voice and opens the door, I will come in and eat with him, and he with me."

Just before the activity, set the paper plates and cups on the table. Begin the activity by gathering students near a door.

Today, you heard that Jesus is the guest we invited into our lives when we asked Him to be our Savior. Revelation 3:20 talks about how we invite Him into every part of our life. **Read the verse.** Today, we'll take turns acting out this verse as we read it. We will need two actors: one person who will represent Jesus and one person to represent each of us. **Assign these roles and put the proper placard on each actor. Have the JESUS actor stand just outside the classroom door.**

We will all say the verse together. When we say "Here I am," the actor who is playing JESUS will point to himself. When we say "I stand at the door and knock," the JESUS actor will knock on the door. When we say "If anyone hears my voice," the actor who is playing US will put his hand to his ear. When we say "and opens the door," the US actor will open the door. When we say "I will come in," the JESUS actor will come inside and close the door. When we say "and eat with him, and he with me," the JESUS actor and US actor will sit at the table and pretend to eat.

Do these actions three or four times, switching roles so more students have an opportunity to participate. Then have students pair up and say the verse to each other.

WEEKLY ASSIGNMENT: Change of Heart

Today in our class, we invited a special guest. This helped us remember how we invited Jesus into our life. We know that Jesus is part of our lives at all times. He never leaves us.

This week, make a special effort to think about Jesus being your special guest. **Pass out sheets of heart stickers so each person has at least five stickers. Staple each sticker sheet to the top of the "C'mon In!" handout.**

Remember how you drew things on your blueprint to represent the things that you turned over to the control of Jesus. This week, let's put into practice your new desire to let Jesus be most important in your life. Hang up your blueprint in your room. Each time you are tempted to let one of the things you drew take control of your time or your thoughts, ask Jesus to take control instead. Each time you let Jesus control it, put a heart sticker beside the thing that you prayed about. For example, if watching television is a problem for you after you come home from school, ask Jesus to help you do your chores first. Then put a heart beside the television and go do your chores. See if you can use all your stickers in one week.

Allow your guest to give his or her comments about the class. Let students ask questions about his or her experience in the classroom, then have them thank the guest for coming.

What a Change!

As you listen to the story, write down any changes you see between Paul's life before he met Jesus and his life after he met Jesus.

The Apostle Paul's Changes	
BEFORE	**AFTER**

My Changes	
BEFORE	**AFTER**

C'mon In!

On this blueprint of a house are several rooms. In the rooms, draw things you own that are important to you. For example, in the garage you might draw a bicycle. Also draw things that you spend a lot of time using. In the family room, you might draw a picture of a VCR or a video-game machine. Draw at least three or four things. A television has already been included in the family room.

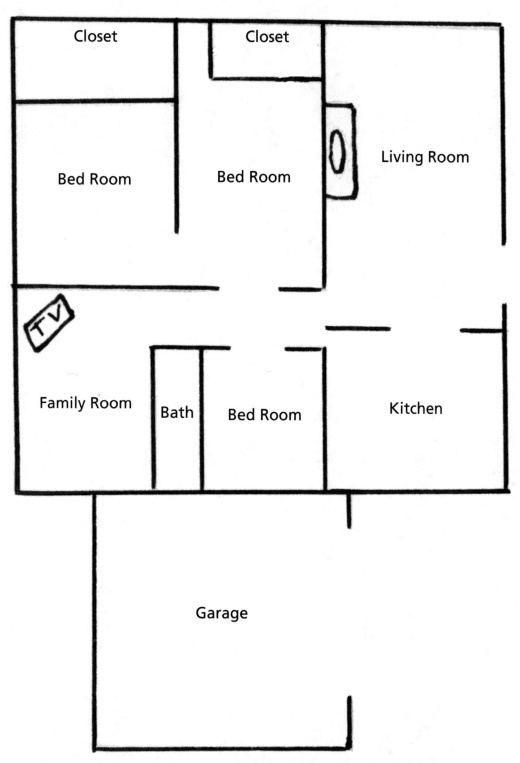

UNIT TWO

The Christian Adventure

BOOK OBJECTIVE	To introduce students to Jesus and the Christian life and to help them begin to grow as believers.
UNIT OBJECTIVE	To introduce students to the basics of the Christian life.
LESSON 5: Spiritual Birthday Party	*Objective:* To help students who have received Christ as their Savior to gain an assurance of their salvation and of the presence of Jesus in their lives. *Application:* To help students demonstrate the certainty of their position in Christ.
LESSON 6: Circle of Life	*Objective:* To help students discover that the indwelling Christ is the key to the Christian life. *Application:* To help students plan ways to allow Christ to control their out-of-control areas.
LESSON 7: Food for Growth	*Objective:* To help students learn the five principles of Christian growth and how they help a believer mature in faith. *Application:* To help students apply the five principles of Christian growth to their daily lives.
LESSON 8: Critical Communication	*Objective:* To help students learn the importance of studying the Bible and praying. *Application:* To help students develop a plan to study the Bible and to have a regular time of prayer.

Drew was a sharp, dedicated high school senior who provided leadership to the youth group in his church. Through the influence of his parents and a good church, he received Christ as a young boy. But like many young people growing up in church, he experienced little spiritual growth.

One summer Drew rededicated his life to Christ, but he still felt something was missing. Today, however, that has changed. His discovery of the Person and power of God's Holy Spirit has transformed him into a joyful Christian and a vibrant witness for Christ.

Drew came to realize that living the Christian life is not simply difficult—it is impossible. Only through the power of the Holy Spirit within us can we possibly have the strength to resist temptation and to make the right choices.

"The message had never reached me that I must let the Lord, in the form of the Holy Spirit, live the Christian life through me," Drew says. "I cannot express the joy I felt when I discovered that the 'burden' of living the Christian life is really no burden at all because the Holy Spirit will live it through me if I invite Him and trust Him to do so."

The Christian life is a great adventure because God loves us and has a wonderful, exciting plan for us. We are not creatures of chance, brought into the world for a meaningless, miserable existence; rather we are people of destiny, created for meaningful, fruitful, and joyful lives.

Your young students can harness this divine power in their lives also. When they do, they may avoid the pitfalls that many youngsters fall into as they mature into adults.

You may also find principles that will help you mature in your life. In this study, you will travel along with your students on an exciting journey through many important scriptural concepts. I want to share with you vital truths that will help you understand and experience the great adventure of the Christian life. I guarantee that, as you and your students apply what you learn in this book to your daily living, your lives will never be the same.

The spiritual wildernesses of your life will diminish in size and frequency. You will learn how to delight in the Lord every day—even when your circumstances are not always delightful. Boredom will become excitement. Hopelessness will become hope. Your walk with God will take on a new dimension of purpose and power because you are allowing the Holy Spirit to do His work in and through your life.

My prayer is that this study will bless and enrich the lives of your students in a dramatic, supernatural way. I encourage you to help them grow toward maturity in Jesus Christ as they become more like Him. The Weekly Assignments will help you implant scriptural principles and habits into their lives. The Lord bless you as you teach the next generation about the exciting Christian adventure!

Spiritual Birthday Party

LESSON PLAN

OBJECTIVE: Students who have received Christ as their Savior will gain an assurance of their salvation and of the presence of Jesus in their lives.

APPLICATION: Students will demonstrate the certainty of their position in Christ.

LESSON PLAN ELEMENT	ACTIVITY	TIME	SUPPLIES
Opening Activity	*How Old Am I?*	7–10	Paper; pencils; birthday hat/birthday party favors/birthday banner
Bible Story—John 3:1–18, the story of Nicodemus	*A Second Birthday*	10–15	Decorated 9"×13" birthday cake; birthday candles; Bible
Lesson Activity	*The "Light" Thing to Do*	7–10	Large candle; matches; *Would You Like to Belong to God's Family?* booklets (optional)
Check for Understanding	*My Spiritual Birthday*	2–3	"Spiritual Birth Certificate" handouts; pencils
Application	*Sealed Up!*	7–10	Bibles; envelopes; index cards; pencils
Memory Verse Activity	*It's a Piece of Cake*	4–7	Knife; paper plates in three different colors; large sheet of paper; marker; chalkboard or poster board
Weekly Assignment	*Sealed for Sure!*	3–5	Envelopes; index cards

Believers in Old Testament times looked forward to the coming of their Messiah. New Testament believers look back to the cross and the resurrection. Both culminate in the unique person of Jesus Christ. Paul writes:

It was through what His Son did that God cleared a path for everything to come to Him—all things in heaven and on earth—for Christ's death on the cross has made peace with God for all by His blood...and now as a result Christ has brought you into the very presence of God, and you are standing there before Him with nothing left against you...; the only condition is that you fully believe the Truth, standing in it steadfast and firm, strong in the Lord, convinced of the Good News that Jesus died for you, and never shifting from trusting Him to save you (Colossians 1:20,22,23, TLB).

Hundreds of millions of people around the world have discovered this marvelous "path" because of Jesus' death on the cross and His bodily resurrection from the dead.

Jesus' death bridged the gulf between the holiness of God and the sinfulness of man. He died to pay the penalty of our sin and rescue us "out of the darkness and gloom of Satan's kingdom" and to bring us "into the Kingdom of [God's] dear Son, who bought our freedom with His blood and forgave us all our sins" (Colossians 1:13,14, TLB). But without His resurrection and ascension, we would have remained under the penalty of death (1 Corinthians 15:17). It is because He has power over death that He can give us eternal life.

To believe in Jesus Christ as the Savior of the world is to believe in a living person. People often ask, "What is the meaning of belief?" *The Amplified New Testament* expresses the full meaning of the term *believe* as "adhere to, trust in, and rely on." The Gospel of John has been called the Gospel of Belief. The word *believe* occurs many times in the book. Chapter 20, verse 31, expresses the purpose of the Gospel of John:

These are written that you may believe that Jesus is the Christ, the Son of God, and that by believing you may have life in His name.

The living Savior, therefore, is the basis for Christian confidence. The resurrection is the foundation of our certainty that we have eternal life in Christ and that we experience daily the indwelling presence of our living Savior.

Your students will be able to live a more joyful Christian life as they gain confidence in what we are promised in Christ. They need to be reassured of God's unconditional and everlasting love for His children. At the same time, be sure to explain that this assurance does not apply to those who are not members of God's family. Be sensitive to where your students are spiritually as you teach this lesson.

LESSON PLAN

OPENING ACTIVITY: How Old Am I?

 Before Class: Put up a birthday banner. Find out the ages of the following, if possible:

- The president
- Your pastor
- The United States of America
- Your state
- The Statue of Liberty
- Your church or school
- Your city
- Yourself, if you want to disclose your age (Be prepared for some outlandish guesses!)

If possible, find the names of two famous people who were born on the day of your class session or a day close to it. This can usually be found in the newspaper. If you don't find someone famous to celebrate, use a friend's name or bring in a stuffed animal. Put on a birthday hat or hold a party favor.

- What do you think I am celebrating today? *(Your birthday; somebody's birthday.)*

Yes, I am celebrating somebody's birthday. Did you know that _____ was born today?

- How old do you think he/she is? *(Allow the children to guess, then reveal the answer.)*

Let's play a game to see how old other people or places are. **Hand out pencils and paper. Number your paper from 1 to 9 and let's see how many ages you get right. As I name each person or place, write down the age you are guessing. Go through the list above. For number nine, ask students to guess the age of the person sitting on their right. When everyone finishes, reveal the correct answers.**

- Why are our birthdays or ages so important to us? *(It is the day we were born. We like to know how long we have lived. We like to have one day when people treat us special.)*

Everyone has a birthday. It was that special day when we were born here on earth. Many of us celebrate this special day with a party, cake, and presents. For some of us, it is the most exciting day of the year. We like people to remember our special day and people like to know how long ago that special day happened. That is why we keep track of our age. But did you know that you have another birthday? Did you also know that this day is very important too? Let's listen to our Bible story to find out what this special second birthday is.

BIBLE STORY: A Second Birthday

It is very exciting to have a birthday and have your friends treat you extra special for one day. One tradition we usually practice during a birthday is having a cake and candles. **Bring out the cake and set it in front of your group. Give each student one candle. If there are more than thirty students in your class, pair students. Otherwise, the cake will have too many candles.**

As I tell the story, think of one fact brought out in this story about your new life in Christ that means a lot to you. After I finish telling the story, each person will put his or her candle on the cake while telling us what means the most to you.

Open your Bible to John 3. Tell this story rather than reading it.

This story took place during the first century when Jesus was living on earth. It is about Nicodemus, who was an important man. In fact, he was part of the most important religious group in the city of Jerusalem—the Pharisees. All the Jewish people looked up to him because of his position. As part of his position, he helped make the rules that his people had to live by.

But there was one thing that bothered Nicodemus. That was the news about Jesus. Jesus had done all kinds of miracles and taught the people in a way that was amazing to Nicodemus. Although Nicodemus had spent a lot of time studying the Scriptures (only the Old Testament was written at this time), Jesus knew more about God's Word than he did. Nicodemus was curious about what Jesus taught. But there was a problem. Most of the Pharisees hated Jesus. They wouldn't like it if Nicodemus was seen visiting Jesus.

That's why Nicodemus came to where Jesus was staying at night. He didn't want his friends to know what he was doing. But he just had to see Jesus.

When he got there, Jesus welcomed him. Nicodemus made an amazing statement. **Read John 3:2.** In other words, Nicodemus wanted to know if Jesus was really the Son of God.

Jesus gave a strange answer. **Read John 3:3.**

Nicodemus asked, **Read John 3:4.**

Jesus explained what He meant. He said something like this. When we are born into the world, we are born with a body. We are born with flesh and bones. But that doesn't mean we can enter God's kingdom. God's kingdom is a spiritual one, not a physical one. Therefore, we have to be "born again" into God's spiritual kingdom. The Holy Spirit gives us a new birth when we confess our sins and ask Jesus to come into our life to pay the penalty for our sins.

When you are born physically, everyone could see that you had been born. You came into the world with a body and you are alive. But when you are born of the Spirit, your new birth is not automatically seen by others. **Read John 3:8.** But your new birth is just as real and permanent as your physical birth.

Jesus said that your physical birth is an earthly event. But your spiritual birth is a heavenly event. That's why it's harder to understand. The only One who can completely understand is Jesus because He came from God and He is God. **Read John 3:13,14.**

Then Jesus gave Nicodemus a promise from God the Father. You probably have memorized this promise. **Have students say John 3:16 together. Then read John 3:17,18.**

The promise from God is that if you believe in Jesus, you will have eternal life. You will be a permanent member of God's family. When you were born into your physical family, you received your parents' DNA. No matter what happens, you will always have their DNA. You are their physical child. That's the same way in God's family. When you received Jesus as your Savior, you received the Holy Spirit in your life as your spiritual DNA. No matter what happens, you will always be part of God's family.

Now let's see what you chose as the most important element of this story for you.

Allow students to come up one at a time and place their candle in the cake as they tell the most important fact in the story for them. Some answers could be: (*I have eternal life. I am part of God's family. We can be born again.*)

- If you were Nicodemus, what would you have asked Jesus? (*Allow students to give personal responses.*)

- Why do you think Jesus welcomed Nicodemus even though Nicodemus was too embarrassed to be seen with Jesus in the daylight? (*Jesus loves everyone, even those who are afraid to admit they want to know Him. Jesus could see Nicodemus's heart.*)

- What was the most important fact that Nicodemus learned that night? (*That he could be born again. That God loves him and wants him to become a believer in Jesus.*)

John chapter 3 doesn't tell us what happened to Nicodemus. Did he ask Jesus to forgive his sins? Did he become a member of God's family?

Later in the Book of John, we learn one more interesting fact about Nicodemus. **Ask a good reader to read John 19:38–42.** I think that Nicodemus overcame his fear of being recognized as a Christian believer. He took the daring step of going with Joseph of Arimathea to bury Jesus. He braved the anger of his Pharisee friends and the presence of soldiers. His faith was out in the open. The Holy Spirit helped him become a visible worker in God's kingdom. Although the Bible doesn't tell us for sure, I think Nicodemus had a spiritual birthday that night!

LESSON ACTIVITY: The "Light" Thing to Do

For this activity, ask another adult to help you counsel any students who indicate that they want to receive Jesus Christ as Savior. You may want to provide a booklet such as *Would You Like to Belong to God's Family?* **to read through with these students.**

Jesus tells us that we must be sorry for our sins and believe in Him. Let's review what a person must do to become a Christian. I'm going to read several Bible verses aloud. After each one, tell me what you think the answer is. **Use these questions to determine what your students understand about becoming a Christian. Discuss any misconceptions they have, always coming back to the clear facts in the Bible.**

1. What must a person do to become a Christian? **Read John 1:12.** *(Receive Jesus Christ as your Savior.)*

2. Who is a person born of when he receives Jesus as his Savior? **Read John 1:13.** *(Of God.)*

3. When you believe in Jesus, what does God take away that is bad for you? **Read John 5:24.** *(Death.)*

This death is spiritual death or permanent separation from God. This verse promises that believers will never be separated from God again. If you are His child, you will always be with Him and will live with Him forever in heaven.

4. What did Jesus do with our sins? **Read 1 Peter 2:24,25.** *(He paid for them on the cross.)*

When Jesus was talking to Nicodemus, He described what it was like to become a new member of God's family. He used a special way to describe it. **Have a good reader read John 3:19–21.**

In these verses, Jesus is the light. He gave us the truth. Truth is like light. It opens our eyes to what's right. Jesus gave us the truth that enabled us to see what God is like and what we must do to become a child of God. If you have never received Jesus as your Savior, you are living in darkness. If you have received Jesus, you are living in the light. Isn't that great?

Dim the lights in the room. Our dark room is like your life if you aren't a member of God's kingdom. Of course, we can't make our room completely dark.

- What would it be like if every bit of light was removed from this room? *(We couldn't see anything. It would be scary. We would bump into things and fall over.)*

None of us has ever seen a place where there was no light. Even in the darkest room, there is still a little light. But the total absence of light would be very terrible.

- How is the absence of light like a person's life who does not believe in God? *(They won't know where to go when they have trouble. They won't be able to see things the way they really are.)*

Jesus is our light. The Bible calls Him the Light of the World. **Light the large tapered candle. Then use it to light the small birthday candles. (If you feel your students can handle it, allow them to light their own candles. But put safety first. Also, watch that your candles don't burn too fast and drip wax all over the cake.)** Isn't it beautiful in here now? Light is so beautiful to watch.

- How is Jesus like this light? *(He shows us God's truth. He is the most beautiful person because He never sinned. He helps us see the way to God.)*

Blow out the candles and turn on the lights. Have you ever received Jesus as your Savior? If you haven't, now is a good time. You can come from darkness to light. You can be a permanent member of God's family. I like to think of this as the "light" thing to do! If you would like to learn more about making this choice, raise your hand and someone will talk with you privately.

Give students a moment to raise their hands. Send these students with your adult

helper for counseling. Continue the lesson with your other students.

CHECK FOR UNDERSTANDING: My Spiritual Birthday
Distribute the "Spiritual Birth Certificate" handouts and pencils.

If you've had a spiritual birth, let's celebrate your spiritual birthday by filling out "Spiritual Birth Certificates." Do you remember the day that you received Jesus as your Savior? Perhaps you can't remember the day or the month, but you can remember the year.

On your Certificate in your best cursive writing, write your full name, the date of your physical birth, and your parents' names. **If students who are adopted or have legal guardians are unsure about who to put in the blanks, have them write the names of those who are responsible for their welfare right now, just as God is the One who takes care of us right now.**

Now write the date you had your spiritual birthday. That is the time when you sincerely made a decision to ask Jesus to be your Savior. **Some students may not remember when they received Jesus as their Savior. Help them recall about the age they were and write that date on their Certificates. As you work with your students, make sure they know the basics of how to become a Christian and that they sincerely made that decision. If some students are not ready to receive Christ, have them leave the Spiritual Birth and Place lines blank, but assure them that they can do this at any time. Give them each a copy of** *Would You Like to Belong to God's Family?* **and encourage them to read it through.**

If you have students who were out of this activity for counseling, make sure they each get a Spiritual Birth Certificate after class and explain what to do with it.

APPLICATION: Sealed Up!
Make sure that the students who went out for counseling are present for this activity. Give each person two envelopes, a pencil, and a card and make sure each person has a Bible. Have students turn to John 10:25–30.

How sure are you that you will always be a member of God's family? Does it ever worry you that maybe you won't make it to heaven? Let me show you some verses that describe how sure you can be. **Have a good reader read John 10:25–30.**

One of Jesus' names is the Good Shepherd. Jesus calls us His sheep. If you believe in Jesus, you are one of His sheep. A shepherd always takes good care of his sheep.

- What do shepherds do to take care of their sheep? *(If they get lost, he finds them. When they are hungry, he leads them to food. When they are thirsty, he leads them to water.)*

- How does Jesus take care of His sheep? *(He protects us. He makes sure we are taken care of. He shows us how to do the right things.)*

Let's look at these verses again. First, write your name on the card I gave you. That represents the fact that God loves you and makes you a part of His family. **Give students time to write.**

Now write "God the Father" on one of the envelopes and "Jesus the Shepherd" on the other envelope. **Give students time to write.**

- In verse 27, what do the sheep do? (*Follow Jesus; listen to His voice.*)

- In verse 28, what does Jesus promise to do for each of His sheep? (*Give them eternal life; make sure no one takes them out of His hand.*)

Demonstrate the activity as you encourage your students to do it also. To show the fact that Jesus makes sure no one takes His sheep, put the card with your name on it into the envelope labeled "Jesus the Shepherd." Seal the envelope to show that you can never be taken out of the hand of Jesus. **Give students time to do this.**

- In verse 29, what does Jesus promise His sheep? (*The Father is greater than all; no one can take them out of the Father's hand.*)

Imagine! Not only are you protected by Jesus, but also by God the Father. To show that this is true, put the envelope containing the card inside the second envelope labeled "God the Father," then seal it. **Give students time to do this.**

Verse 29 says that the Father is greater or stronger than all. Since you are protected by both God the Father and Jesus the Shepherd, no one can take you away from them. You are safely sealed into God's family.

- How does it make you feel to know that God cares that much about you and what happens to you? (*Allow students to respond.*)

MEMORY VERSE ACTIVITY: It's a Piece of Cake

1 John 5:13—"I write these things to you who believe in the name of the Son of God so that you may know that you have eternal life."

> *Before Class:* Cut the birthday cake into pieces to serve your students. Place the pieces on the plates, making sure each color of plate is represented evenly. Draw a game board with 16 squares (4 across by 4 down) on the large sheet of paper so that a plate can fit on each square. Place the paper on a large table.

Divide the class into three teams. Give each team member a piece of cake with the same color of plate. Instruct them not to eat it. Position the students around the table in team groups. Write 1 John 5:13 on a board or poster.

We learned in our lesson today that a Christian can know that he or she has eternal life because of our spiritual birth. This verse tells us this very important truth. Let's read it together. **Read 1 John 5:13 together several times.**

We are going to play "It's a Piece of Cake" to help us learn this verse. This game is like Tic-Tac-Toe. I will read the verse to you, but I will leave out a word. Your team needs to tell me which word I left out. If your team is correct, one team member will put his piece of cake on one of the game board squares. If the team misses the word, the turn passes to the next team. Teams continue taking turns until a team has three pieces of cake in a row—horizontally, vertically, or diagonally.

When the game is finished, have individuals say the verse out loud and end with the group saying it together. Close by celebrating "spiritual birthdays," eating the cake, and thanking Jesus for giving us eternal life.

WEEKLY ASSIGNMENT: Sealed for Sure!

Don't you wish every member of God's family knew about God's promise to give him or her eternal life—for sure? Perhaps you know Christians who aren't sure if they will go to heaven when they die. Let's share the Good News with them!

Distribute two envelopes and an index card to each student. Have students write "John 10:25–30" on the card, and write "Jesus the Shepherd" on one envelope and "God the Father" on the other.

You can demonstrate this activity to people who believe in Jesus as their Savior. First make sure that this person has received Jesus as Savior. You could ask, "Have you ever prayed and asked Jesus to forgive all your sin because He died on the cross to pay for them? Do you know for sure that you are part of God's family?" If the person says yes, write his or her name on the card. Then go through the demonstration like we did earlier. Read the verses from your Bible. The reference is written on the card so you won't forget.

Close in prayer, thanking God for His protection and love.

Certification of Vital Record

Spiritual
Birth Certificate

Name: _____ _____ _____
             (LAST)   (FIRST)   (MIDDLE)

Date of physical birth: _____

Place of physical birth: _____

Mother: _____

Father: _____

Date of spiritual birth: _____

Place of spiritual birth: _____

Spiritual Father: God, the Almighty Creator of the universe

*"I write these things to you who believe in the name of the Son of God
so that you may* know *that you have eternal life."*

1 JOHN 5:13

LESSON 6

Circle of Life

LESSON PLAN

OBJECTIVE: Students will discover that the indwelling Christ is the key to the Christian life.

APPLICATION: Students will plan ways to allow Christ to control their out-of-control areas.

LESSON PLAN ELEMENT	ACTIVITY	TIME	SUPPLIES
Opening Activity	*"I See You"*	7–10	Two slips of paper; blanket; marker
Bible Story—Philippians 4:13 and the story of John Newton	*A "New" Newton*	10–15	Bible; words for *Amazing Grace*
Lesson Activity	*In Which Circle Are You?*	7–10	Bibles; "Life Circles" handouts; pencils
Check for Understanding	*Life Circles*	3–5	"Life Circles" handouts; pencils
Application	*A Prescription for Worldliness*	7–10	3 clean prescription bottles; 3 slips of paper; marker; photocopy of script; paper; pencils
Memory Verse Activity	*Memory Circle*	3–5	
Weekly Assignment	*Control Check-Up*	3–5	"Life Circles" handouts

In every life, there is a throne, a control center—the intersection of one's intellect, emotions, and will. Either self or Christ is on that throne. That is what the Christian life is all about—keeping Christ on the throne of our life. We do this when we understand how to walk in the control and power of the Holy Spirit, for the Holy Spirit came to glorify Christ by enabling the believer to live a holy life and to be a fruitful witness for our dear Savior.

Many people, however, have misconceptions about the Christian life. Some argue that once they have received Jesus Christ into their lives by faith, it is up to them in their own strength to live a life pleasing to God. Others believe that Christ has entered their lives merely to help them live and work for God's glory. These ideas of Christian living look good on the surface, but each contains a weakness that actually undermines the basis of vital Christian living.

Someone said, "The Christian life is not difficult—it is impossible." Only one person has lived the Christian life, and that was Jesus Christ. Today, He desires to go on living His life through—not alongside of or as an observer to—Christians by the power of the Holy Spirit who lives in them. In the preface of *Letters to Young Churches*, his translation of a portion of the New Testament, J. B. Phillips writes:

> The great difference between present-day Christianity and that of which we read in these letters is that to us it is primarily a performance, while to them it was a real experience. We are apt to reduce the Christian religion to a code, or at best a rule of heart and life. To those men it is quite plainly the invasion of their lives by a new quality of life altogether. They do not hesitate to describe this as Christ "living" in them.

Before His death, Christ told His disciples that it was best for Him to leave them so that the Spirit of God might come to dwell in each of them (John 14:16–20; 16:7). In other words, Christ was physically departing from His disciples so that He might always be present within each of them through His Spirit.

Today, when a person places his faith in Christ, Jesus comes to dwell in that person by means of the Holy Spirit (Romans 8:9). Christ's purpose for dwelling in us is to live His life through us. Yet sadly, many Christians are trying to operate on their own finite ability instead of in Christ's infinite power.

You may then wonder, "How can I experience this victorious life of Christ?" The answer is through understanding the three types of people in the world: the non-Christian (natural man), the spiritual Christian, and the worldly or carnal Christian. The natural man is the person who has never invited Christ to be a part of his life. The spiritual Christian is one who has turned his life over to our Lord Jesus Christ and is now living in the resurrected power of Christ. The worldly Christian is one who has let self rule in his life and therefore gets caught up in the things of this world.

In this lesson, your students will learn the differences between each of these types of people. Then they will decide which "circle" they are in. Finally, your students will discover the solution to living a worldly life—allowing Jesus to take control of every part of their life.

Before you teach this lesson, make sure you have also put Christ in the control center of your life. As you study the lesson, apply the scriptural principles to your life before you teach them to your students.

DING! DONG!

LESSON PLAN

OPENING ACTIVITY: "I See You"

Before Class: Write all of the following words on each of the two slips of paper:

- Happy
- Selfish
- Angry
- Mean
- Sad
- Proud
- Kind
- Jealous
- Bad talking
- Impatient
- Generous
- Peaceful

Discuss what happened when your students shared their envelopes with other Christians. Talk about how exciting it is to be sure that God will always love you and that you are going to heaven.

Divide your class into two teams. Assign one person from each team to be a blanket-holder. Now that you have Christ in your life, you have two choices: either Christ can control your life, or you yourself can keep trying to control your own life. The results of either choice can be seen through your actions. Let's play a game to see some characteristics of a self-controlled or worldly life and a Christ-controlled life.

Have the students sit on the floor in their team groups, with the teams facing each other. When the game starts, two students will hold a blanket vertically between the two groups and drop it at your signal.

I have two slips of paper with the same characteristics written on each of them. These characteristics are either the actions of a self-controlled Christian or a Christ-controlled Christian. One of your team members will be responsible for acting out one of the characteristics. To start the game, you will pick one person from your team to be the actor. The two students I have selected will hold up the blanket. I will show the actors one of the characteristics on their slip of paper to act out. This blanket will be like a theater curtain that keeps the audience from seeing the stage. When the blanket drops, both actors will act out their characteristic without saying any words. The actors may not have the same word, so be sure you look at your team's actor.

Give each slip to the actor from each team. Hold up the blanket. Have actors walk to the opposite side of the blanket and face their team. Point out a different characteristic to each actor. When you say "go," the students drop the blanket and the actors begin. The first team that guesses the correct characteristic wins the point. Keep score of the number of points for each team. When a team guesses correctly, ask them this question:

- Which person would display this characteristic in his life—a Christ-controlled life or a self-controlled (worldly) life?

Happy *(Christ-controlled)*   Selfish *(self-controlled)*

Mean *(self-controlled)*   Sad *(self-controlled)*

Kind *(Christ-controlled)*   Jealous *(self-controlled)*

Impatient (*self-controlled*)   Generous (*Christ-controlled*)

Angry (*self-controlled*)   Proud (*self-controlled*)

Bad talking (*self-controlled*)   Peaceful (Christ-controlled)

When the activity is finished, say: Think about yourself. Which one of these characteristics do you think you display most often? Let's listen to a story about a famous man who started out living a self-controlled life and then lived a Christ-controlled life.

BIBLE STORY: A "New" Newton

Write the words to *Amazing Grace* on your chalkboard.

> *Amazing grace, how sweet the sound*
> *That saved a wretch like me.*
> *I once was lost but now am found.*
> *Was blind, but now I see.*

To begin this activity, sing *Amazing Grace* together.

When we were singing this song, did you notice the words? Did you pay any attention to what they said? Let's read through them together.

Read through the words with your students.

Teaching Tip: If some of your students do not know the meanings of the following words, give their definitions:

Grace: getting something good that you don't deserve

Wretch: a despicable, miserable person

Lost: cannot find the way to God

Blind: does not understand the truth about God

- What do the words of this song mean to you? (*Allow students to respond.*)

- What kind of a person do you think would write the words to this song? (*Allow students to give responses.*)

Divide and group your students into the following acting teams. Have groups briefly decide on what they will do to act out their parts. Possible actions for each group are given in italics following the group names.

The Sea Storm (*Hand waving like waves; thunder crashes; wind blowing.*)

The Crowd (*Shouting "the old converted sea captain"; "yeah, John"; "praise God."*)

The Slaves (*Crying; moaning; bent over working hard.*)

When I tell this story, the acting groups will act out their parts. When I get to the part where your group should act, I will point to your group.

The man who wrote *Amazing Grace*, John Newton, lived from 1725 to 1807. That was about the same time the Declaration of Independence was written and the thirteen colonies fought the Revolutionary War to become the United States of America. But John Newton grew up in England, the country the colonists were fighting against. His mother loved God and wanted her son to grow up to be a preacher. But she died when John was little.

John's father was a sea captain. John decided to follow in his father's footsteps, so he joined the Royal Navy. **Point to Sea Storm acting group.** But he didn't like the rules of Navy life. He went AWOL (absent without leave), was caught, and beaten by the authorities. Eventually, he got out of the Navy.

What John wanted to do was to live just as he pleased—doing any kind of sinful pleasure that he wanted to do. He got a job working for a slave trader on the western coast of Africa.

During this time, slavery was still practiced in the United States. Slave ships would sail to Africa, pick up a cargo of slaves, and take them to America to sell. **Point to Slave acting group.** The slave trader treated John very badly. After a while, John ended up on the Island of Plaintains where he worked on a lemon plantation (a large farm that used slaves). His clothes were rags; he had to beg for food. After a year, he escaped from the island.

Then he began working as a sailor on a ship. Eventually, he worked his way up so that he became the captain of a slave ship. **Point to Slave acting group.** John did this for six years.

During the time he was a sailor, he began thinking about his life and the kind of person he had become. One day a severe storm battered the ship. **Point to Sea Storm acting group.** Although he was an experienced sailor, that terrible storm scared him. **Point to Sea Storm acting group.** That night, he asked Jesus to be his Savior.

John's life began to change. Although he still worked as a captain on a slave ship for six more years, Jesus began changing John's heart. John began to hate slavery. In fact, he grew to hate it so much that he quit being a slave-ship captain and began going around speaking against slavery. In time, he fell in love and got married and then trained to be a preacher. His mother's prayers had finally been answered!

Whenever he preached, he drew large crowds. People called him the "old converted sea captain." **Point to Crowd acting group.** He also wrote many hymns; one was *Amazing Grace*. It is one of the most loved songs in the church today.

When he got very old, people told him he should retire because of bad health. He said, "My memory is nearly gone, but I remember two things: That I am a great sinner and that Christ is a great Savior."

Now let's think of the words to *Amazing Grace* again.

- What can you see in these words that tells us what John Newton thought about Jesus? *(That he didn't deserve to be a Christian, but Jesus saved him anyway. That Jesus can make a sinner good again.)*

Humans cannot do anything good on their own. All our power to do good comes from Jesus. **Read 2 Peter 1:3.** This verse tells us that Jesus gives us everything we need to live a good life. It is His power that allows us to do what's right. John Newton received power to change from a slave trader to a preacher. That's an amazing change. In our Lesson Activity, we will learn what it means to have Christ's power in our life.

LESSON ACTIVITY: In Which Circle Are You?

Use the following three diagrams as an example for this activity.

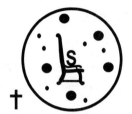
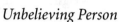

Unbelieving Person

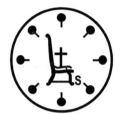

Spiritual Christian

Worldly Christian

Distribute the "Life Circles" handouts and pencils, and make sure every student has a Bible.

The Bible tells us that there are three kinds of people. The circles on your worksheet represent the three different kinds of people. Do you see the throne in the center of each circle? That throne represents the control center in a person's life. A control center shows who is running that life.

Let me give you an example. Andy is the best baseball player on his school's team. His batting average is very high and he is an excellent catcher. His teammates admire him for his talent. When Andy wakes up in the morning, he thinks about baseball. He thinks about baseball all day long. He loves to hear people tell him how good he is.

One day, Andy's mother asks him to babysit his two-year-old sister while she runs to the grocery store. Just after she leaves, Andy's friends knock on the door and want him to practice catching. Andy takes his two-year-old sister with him to the park. Soon he and his friends are so involved in their practice that Andy forgets to watch his sister. She wanders off into the street.

Do you see that Andy has a control problem in his life? He knows he's supposed to be watching his sister, but his desire to play ball wins out. He doesn't do what's right. He thinks about himself first.

What we put on the throne of our life is very important. There are two possibilities of who can be on the throne, or control center, of your life—yourself or Jesus.

- Which one of these two possibilities did Andy have on the throne of his life? *(Self.)*

- What can happen when a person is controlled by his own selfish interests? *(He can get into trouble. He won't do the right things.)*

Now let's look at the circles on your worksheet. The first circle represents the life of a person who has never received Christ as his Savior. He is not a Christian. Christ stands outside the door of his life, wanting to come in. To show that Jesus is not in this person's life, draw a cross outside the circle. **Give students a moment to place a cross outside the circle.**

The chair or throne represents the "control center" of your life. Just as space ships are controlled by NASA in Houston, your life is controlled by something too.

- What do you think a nonbeliever is controlled by? *(Himself.)*

Since Jesus is not in the nonbeliever's life, it cannot be Jesus. The truth is that a nonbeliever tries to control his own life. Let's use an "S" to represent that this person has "self" in control of his life. He does what he wants to do no matter who it hurts or how wrong it is. Draw an "S" on the throne. **Give students a moment to draw an "S."**

- What was John Newton's life like before he became a Christian? *(He was mean to people. He wanted to make money so badly that he would do anything to get it. He was unhappy.)*

John Newton's life shows us that without Christ, we cannot do what's right. Our life is a mess. Let's see what kind of characteristics a person who does not know Christ displays in his life.

Ask several students to read the following verses aloud. Discuss each characteristic the verse points out. After each one, have students write the phrase on the lines beside the first circle. Then have students write "Unbelieving Person" across the top of the circle.

1 Corinthians 2:14—*(cannot understand God)*

Romans 6:6—*(slave to sin)*

Ephesians 2:1—*(spiritually dead in sin)*

Jeremiah 17:9—*(deceitful heart)*

John 3:36—*(does not believe in Jesus)*

- What kinds of things do you think a person who doesn't know Jesus will do? *(Help students come up with answers such as: swearing, stealing, taking drugs, hating others, never going to church.)*

Draw one or two of these actions inside the first circle. For example, you could draw a face with a hateful expression on it or a syringe to represent drugs. **Give students time to draw.**

The next circle represents the person who has asked Jesus to be his Savior and allows Jesus to control his life. We will call this person a "spiritual Christian." Write that at the top of this circle. **Give students time to write.** Now self is not on the throne. To show this, draw an "S" inside the circle but not on the throne. **Allow students to draw.** Jesus controls this person's life, so draw a cross on the throne. **Give students time to draw.** When we let Jesus control our life, God makes our life wonderful, exciting, and adventurous. The Bible gives us characteristics of a spiritual person. **Read Galatians 5:22,23. Have students write the characteristics (fruits of the Spirit) beside the second circle.**

- What kinds of things would a person do who had these qualities in his life? Give me some examples. *(Love other people. Help others. Be happy. Not fight or argue.)*

Inside the second circle, draw a picture of something someone would do who is letting Jesus control his life. Examples could be helping an elderly person, setting the table for your mother, or giving money at church. **Give students time to draw.**

Can you see what a difference it makes to have Jesus control your life? But, sadly, many Christians slip up and take Jesus off the throne of their life and put "self" back on.

The third circle represents the person who is a member of God's family but doesn't let Jesus control his life. We could call this person a worldly Christian because he is doing the bad things offered by the world's way of living. Write "worldly Christian" over the third circle. **Give students time to write.**

Although Jesus is still in this person's life, He is not on the throne controlling that person's actions. **Instruct students to draw a cross inside the circle but not on the throne.**

- Where do you think the "S" or "self" is in this person's life? *(On the throne.)*

Have students draw an "S" on the throne in the third circle.

Let's look up some Bible verses that describe what the worldly Christian is like. What word or phrase would you use to describe the person in each of these verses? **Read each verse and allow volunteers to answer. Bring out the following answers. Instruct students to write the characteristics next to the third circle.**

- 1 Corinthians 3:1–3—*(He's a spiritual baby; jealous; quarrels; acts like the world.)*

- Galatians 5:19–21—*(He hates others; worships idols; has sex outside of marriage; gets terribly angry; is selfish; gets drunk; is envious of others.)*

How would a person your age act if he had "self" on the throne? He would probably let video games control his free time or he would frequently get angry with his brothers and sisters. He would not read his Bible or pray. Do you see that the worldly Christian acts a lot like a person who does not believe in Jesus? That's because self is controlling both of their lives. Draw something in the third circle to represent a Christian who is trying to control his own life. For example, you could draw someone who is angry or very sad. **Give students time to draw.**

When we control our own life instead of letting Jesus control it, our life becomes a mess.

- Why do you think there is so much difference between the self-controlled life and the life that is controlled by Jesus? *(God makes the difference. Jesus makes our lives better. Jesus helps us do what's right.)*

- How can you tell which circle you are in right now? *(By how I act. If there is sin in my life, I'm not letting Jesus control my life. When I get selfish and want what I want no matter what, I'm not in the Spiritual Christian circle.)*

CHECK FOR UNDERSTANDING: Life Circles

Because the Bible tells us that there are only three types of people in the world, your life is like one of these circles. You are either a person who doesn't believe in God, a person who believes in God and lets Jesus control his life, or a person who believes in God but wants to run his own life.

Decide which circle best describes your life right now. Draw an "X" on that circle. For example, if you have never made a decision to follow Christ, draw an "X" on the Unbelieving Person. If you think you are a Spiritual Christian, draw an "X" on that circle. If you think you are a Worldly Christian, draw an "X" on that circle. This is a private activity. Your decision is between you and God. Therefore, do not look at your neighbor's paper. **Give students a few moments to do this.**

If you are not a Christian and you would like to make a decision to follow Christ, see me after class and I will tell you how you can become a member of God's family.

If you are a Christian, you will find that many times in your life you will move from the spiritual circle to the worldly one. That happens to every Christian when he or she sins. In our next activity, we will find out how we can go from the worldly circle to the spiritual circle when we sin.

APPLICATION: A Prescription for Worldliness

Before Class: On a slip of paper, write this line for a student to read: "As I listened to this lesson, I realized that my life is not controlled by Christ. What can I do to solve this problem?" Write the following prescriptions on small slips of paper and put in empty prescription bottles:

Prescription One:
To rid yourself of worldliness or self-control, you must first confess your sins.

Prescription Two:
To rid yourself of worldliness or self-control, you must surrender your throne to Christ.

Prescription Three:
The last thing you must do to rid yourself of worldliness is to recognize that Christ is now on the throne of your life.

Put the three bottles in front of the room. Choose a student to play the character of Sam, and give him a copy of his line to read. Have the assigned student help you present the following skit.

Teacher: **Hi, Sam! Why do you look so troubled?**

(Have student read his line.)

Teacher: **I have just the answer to your problem. Let's look at the three following prescriptions to worldliness or a self-controlled life. Take out the first prescription and read it for us.** *(Allow the student to do this.)*

Teacher: **The first thing you must do is confess to God that you have been ruling your own life.** *(Read 1 John 1:9.)* **This verse tells us that when we confess our sin, God will forgive us and take the sin away.** *(You can choose to have the student pretend to confess his sin.)*

Let's look at the second prescription. *(Have the student take out the prescription from the second jar and read it.)*

Teacher: **This means that you need to voluntarily give everything to Christ and allow Him to control all parts of your life. Paul describes this in Romans 12:1,2.** *(Read verses.)*

(Have the student open the third prescription and read it.)

Teacher: **The final step is very important. You need to believe that Christ is in control now and allow Him to control your life.**

Allow the student to sit down. Distribute copies of the "Life Circles" handout and look at the "Prescription for Worldliness" chart. Make sure students have pencils.

Let's take a few moments to check our lives. First, bow your head and pray while examining your attitude. Ask yourself this question: Do I honestly want Christ to control my life? If the answer is no, then ask God to change your heart. **Give students time to reflect and pray.**

Now open your eyes and look at the handout I gave you. In the first section, list areas of your life that you know are not under Christ's control. They could be things like bad language, TV habits, the kinds of games you play, disobedience to parents or teachers, or disrespect for your brothers and sisters. Take time to let God bring to mind the areas that you are trying to control yourself and write them down in the left column. **Give students a few minutes to do this.**

Now close your eyes and confess these areas to God. Ask Him to reveal to you ways to bring these areas under His control. **Give students time to do this. They may have difficulty seeing solutions to some problems. Circulate and help those who are struggling to find solutions. Possibilities include:** *(Ask God to help you when you feel yourself getting mad. Quit listening to shows that have bad language in them. Thank God every day for your brother or sister.)*

Write in the second column the things that God has brought to mind that can help you bring these areas under His control. Then close your eyes and ask God to help you in these areas. **Give students time to think and pray.**

Now let's learn a memory verse that will help us remember to put Christ on the throne of our lives.

MEMORY VERSE ACTIVITY: Memory Circle

Philippians 4:13—"I can do everything through him who gives me strength."

Write the verse on the chalkboard, then read it aloud. This verse is talking about Jesus. He's the One who gives us strength to do the right things. That's what we learned in our Life Circles. One way to help us remember to keep Jesus on the throne of our life is by memorizing Bible verses. They help us obey Jesus. Right now, let's make a Memory Circle to memorize our verse for today.

Sit in a big circle. Begin clapping in rhythm as a group. Then say one word of the verse along with each clap. Do this several times, then erase the verse on the board. Clap and say the verse in rhythm several more times by using different voice patterns such as whispering, singing, and using a high voice or low voice.

WEEKLY ASSIGNMENT: Control Check-Up

Look at the "Prescription for Worldliness" chart you worked on in class. Notice that there is a place to mark changes in your life. This week, work on the areas that you wrote about on this chart. Write notes for each day. See if you can have a Christ-controlled week. Bring your sheets next week for our sharing time.

Life Circles

_____
_____
_____
_____
_____

_____
_____
_____
_____
_____
_____
_____
_____

_____
_____
_____
_____
_____
_____
_____
_____

Prescription for Worldliness

In the first column, write down areas where you need to ask Jesus to help you. In the second column, write down ways you could ask Jesus to help you. Then this week mark any changes you see in your life each day. For example, you could write something like this:

Monday: After I prayed, Jesus helped me treat my little brother with kindness. Tuesday: I blew it. I had a fight with my brother.
Wednesday: I asked Jesus to help me stay calm when my brother was bugging me. And He did!

Areas that I need to bring under Christ's control	Ways that God has shown me to bring these areas under Christ's control

Changes in my life this week

Mon.	
Tues.	
Wed.	
Thurs.	
Fri.	
Sat.	
Sun.	

Food for Growth

LESSON PLAN

OBJECTIVE: Students will learn the five principles of Christian growth and how they help a believer mature in faith.

APPLICATION: Students will apply the five principles of Christian growth to their daily lives.

LESSON PLAN ELEMENT	ACTIVITY	TIME	SUPPLIES
Opening Activity	*First Foods*	7–10	6 jars of baby food[1]; permanent marker; paper; pencils
Bible Story—John 18, Peter betrays Christ	*Betrayal!*	10–15	Bible; sticks and twigs; red, yellow, and orange cellophane; adult storyteller in biblical costume
Lesson Activity	*Spiritual Food Groups*	7–10	Labels from boxes or cans of food[2]; chalk
Check for Understanding	*Check It Out!*	3–5	"Spiritual Growth Groups" handouts; pencils
Application	*Growing Up Strong*	7–10	"Spiritual Growth Groups" handouts; pencils
Memory Verse Activity	*Memory Mix Up!*	3–5	30 squares of paper, of two different colors (60 total); marker
Weekly Assignment	*A Great Plan*	3–5	"Spiritual Growth Groups" handouts

1 Use baby foods that are easy to identify by taste, such as banana, applesauce, corn, spinach, or green beans. Do not use double flavors such as macaroni/cheese or chicken/applesauce.

2 Cut labels from various food containers. Provide labels from foods that represent the five food groups in the chart. Bring enough labels so that each student can have at least two. It is not necessary to bring the food itself, just the label.

Y ou made the most important decision of your life when you chose to receive Jesus Christ as your Savior and Lord. At that moment, you were born into God's family, and you received everything you need to live the abundant Christian life.

But that does not mean you are as spiritually mature as someone who has walked with Christ for many years. The Christian life is a process that begins with an act of faith and continues by faith.

What do you suppose would happen to a child who doesn't grow properly physically? I am sure you have children in your class who may not be getting the right nutrition. How about the child's emotional growth? This is an even more serious problem for many children today. And last, how about his or her spiritual maturity? Just as physical life requires air, food, water, and rest, spiritual life requires certain things for growth and development. This lesson is designed to help your students grow spiritually as well as physically and mentally.

This lesson deals with five principles of Christian growth. The first two, *We must study God's Word* and *We must pray,* help us deepen our relationship with God. These involve our vertical relationship with God. Through the Bible, God communicates to us; through prayer, we communicate with Him.

The next two principles, *We must fellowship with other Christians* and *We must witness for Christ,* help us reach out to others. They relate to our horizontal relationship with others. In fellowship, we communicate with other Christians about our Savior and the bond He gives us with one another. In witnessing, we communicate with non-Christians. We tell them about Jesus, what He has done for us, and what He desires to do for them.

Principle five, *We must obey God,* is the core of growth. As we obey Him, we experience increasing joy, peace, and fellowship with the Lord Jesus Christ and fellow believers. We also become increasingly mature in our Christian walk.

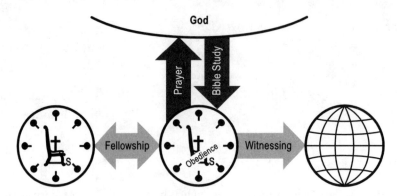

If your students follow these principles, you can be sure that they will grow toward spiritual maturity in Christ. They will learn how to avoid many of the pitfalls that many people experienced in their growing-up years who were not taught to consistently grow spiritually.

LESSON PLAN

OPENING ACTIVITY: First Foods

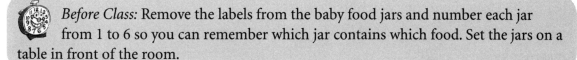
Before Class: Remove the labels from the baby food jars and number each jar from 1 to 6 so you can remember which jar contains which food. Set the jars on a table in front of the room.

Talk with your students about how they allowed Christ to control the out-of-control areas in their lives. Give suggestions about how they can let Christ control these areas even more fully. If a student gives a good example of how he or she let Christ control an area, compliment him or her and suggest that other students write it down on their worksheets.

Hold up a jar of baby food.

- How many of you have ever tasted baby food? *(Some of your students will probably say they have.)*

Probably everyone in this room tasted baby food when they were babies. It is the first food besides milk and rice cereal that most people taste. Let's see if you can identify the flavors of these baby foods.

Give each person six toothpicks, paper, and pencil. Have students number 1 to 6 on their papers. Then allow them to taste and make a guess by writing the flavor on their paper next to the corresponding number on the jar. If they need a second taste, caution students to always use a clean toothpick. If some students feel squeamish about tasting the baby food, have them smell each jar to identify the flavor.

When everyone has finished their taste test, identify each flavor. Have the students check their answers.

That was a fun and interesting activity.

- What are some characteristics of baby food that you noticed in your taste test? *(It doesn't have much taste. The food is smooth and easy to swallow.)*

Now that we're grown up, we turn up our noses at baby food. But most of us liked it at one time in our lives. We enjoyed baby food because our bodies were made for "first foods." Babies can't swallow chunky food; they'll choke on it. And their taste buds haven't been fully developed yet, so they enjoy bland foods.

As a baby gets older, he stops eating baby food and begins eating regular food. He doesn't need baby food anymore. We'd think it was strange if someone at our school brought a bottle of milk and two jars of baby food for lunch. We would not think it was tasty if the school cafeteria set out jars of baby food for us to eat.

Just as we need physical food to help our bodies grow, we need spiritual food to help us grow spiritually. The Bible tells us that new Christians eat spiritual baby food. **Read 1 Peter 2:2.** Reading the Word of God helps us grow spiritually.

The sad fact is that many Christians never get past the "baby food" stage. They're still eating "spiritual baby food" even though they've been Christians for many years. Let's listen to our Bible story about someone who did this.

BIBLE STORY: Betrayal!

 Before Class: For this activity, ask another adult to dress up like Peter and come to your classroom to tell the story. Or you may want to dress up yourself by putting on a headscarf and robe at the appropriate time.

Build a fake campfire in an out-of-the-way corner of your classroom large enough to allow your students to sit in a circle around it to listen to the story. Arrange sticks and twigs in crisscross fashion. Tuck pieces of red, yellow, and orange cellophane into the sticks to resemble flames.

Teaching Tip: If appropriate, build your campfire outside for heightened realism. Also, you could put a lit flashlight under the pile of sticks to make the cellophane "flames" light up.

Begin the class in a part of the room that does not have the campfire.

If you don't exercise your muscles every day, your muscles will get weak. If you don't eat foods with vitamins and minerals every day, your body won't grow as well and you will get weak. Then if you try out for the basketball or soccer team, you won't be able to do as well. You'll tire out and will not have enough energy.

What do you think happens to people who believe in Jesus but don't grow spiritually? What happens to believers who know Jesus but still keep eating "spiritual baby food"? They become spiritually weak.

One thing I especially like about reading the Bible is that it shows us the good and bad actions of people. The good actions show us what God can do through us. The bad actions show us what happens if we don't grow healthy in our spirits. Using those examples, we can avoid doing those bad things.

Move your students to the campfire and have them sit cross-legged around it on the floor. Introduce "Peter."

Today, we have a guest storyteller. The apostle Peter is going to tell us a story about his experiences with Jesus. You can find this story in chapter 18 of the Book of John. Peter was a great man. Jesus picked him to be one of the disciples. Jesus had a lot of confidence in Peter. But Peter still failed when he didn't follow God's leading. Sometimes Peter tried to do things on his own. He let "self" control his life rather than Jesus. He is here today to tell us about a time when he was spiritually weak. Let's imagine that we are in the Palestine countryside many years ago and hear what Peter has to say.

Allow your storyteller to tell the following story in his own words.

It's been about twenty years since I last saw Jesus. But I can still imagine His face as clearly as I can see all of you right now. I loved Him so much. I love Him even more now. I know He is in my life.

But there was one time when I really failed Jesus, a time when He needed me. It's hard for me to talk about it even after all these years.

Let me start my story by explaining something about myself. One problem I've always had is thinking that I can handle anything on my own without God's help. Does that idea ever bother you? This attitude got me into trouble a lot of times.

The other disciples and I had been with Jesus day and night for three years. Then Jesus started telling us that He was going away to a place where we couldn't follow Him. Of course, He was talking about heaven. What He was trying to make us understand was that He was going to die.

One night, we ate the Last Supper we ever had with Jesus. We knew something was up. Jesus seemed very sad. Of course, now I know that He was thinking about His death on the cross the next day.

When Jesus started talking about going away, I said, "Lord, why can't I follow you now? I will lay down my life for you." I had good intentions, but I was trying to follow Jesus by using my own strength. That never works.

Jesus said, "Will you really lay down your life for me? I tell you the truth, before the rooster crows, you will disown me three times!" Jesus knew what I was going to do.

But I didn't believe that I could ever do something so terrible. Not me! I was loyal to Jesus. There was no way that I would ever tell anyone that I didn't know who Jesus was. I'd die for Him if I had to.

Not long after that, things started to get ugly. You've probably heard the story of what happened. Jesus went to a garden to pray to prepare Himself for the hard times ahead of Him. Instead of helping Him, all of us disciples fell asleep. I was pretty embarrassed about that!

Then suddenly, soldiers with torches and lanterns and weapons surrounded Jesus to arrest Him!

I really got mad! (Not a good thing to do!) I remembered my promise to lay down my life for Jesus. I wasn't going to let anyone take Him away. So I pulled out my sword and cut off a servant's ear. Just like that.

Jesus said, "Put your sword away! Shall I not drink the cup the Father has given me?" I still didn't understand that God the Father had sent Jesus to die for the world. But Jesus knew. No one could hurt Jesus unless Jesus let him do it because Jesus has the power of God. Jesus reached up and healed the man's ear. In an instant!

Then the soldiers and religious leaders took Jesus away. All the other disciples ran away scared, but John and I followed the soldiers and Jesus.

It was still very dark when we arrived at a courtyard surrounded by a wall. The soldiers took Jesus inside, but the guards at the gate wouldn't let me enter. John knew the high priest, so he got permission for me to go in. The girl on duty at the gate said, "You are not one of his disciples, are you?"

She thought I was a follower of Jesus! I panicked. I didn't want anyone to know that I was one of His disciples, so I said, "I am not."

It was really cold that night. Some people had built a fire for warmth, so I went closer to it. I could see what the soldiers were doing to Jesus. They were asking Him questions and someone slapped Him on the face! He was tied up so He couldn't protect Himself.

I couldn't believe what they were doing. What if they arrested me too?

While I was thinking, someone standing beside me asked, "You are not one of his disciples, are you?"

Right away, I said, "I am not."

Then a man spoke up who was a relative of the person whose ear I cut off. He said, "Didn't I see you with him in the olive grove?"

I was so scared that I denied I even knew Jesus! As soon as the words came out of my mouth, I heard the rooster crow. The horizon was beginning to get light because the sun was coming up.

At that moment, Jesus turned His head and looked straight at me. I could see the pain in His eyes. I remembered what He had said I would do. "Before the rooster crows, you will disown me three times."

That's what I had done! I felt so low. I had deserted my Lord. I had done what no loyal friend should ever do! I went outside the gate and I cried and cried.

The next day the religious leaders had Jesus put to death. Those were dark days indeed. But then Jesus arose from the dead and our hopes were alive once more! But I didn't think Jesus could ever forgive me for what I had done. I had denied Him three times!

Then one day before He went back to heaven, Jesus said something very special to me. Three times, He asked me if I loved Him. Three times, I answered, "Yes, Lord, you know that I love you."

Then Jesus gave me a most important job to do. "Feed my sheep," He said. He wanted me to help believers grow spiritually! Jesus trusted me! He had forgiven me.

Now I know how I can stay true to Jesus. I let His Spirit help me grow spiritually. I must continue to grow to be more like Jesus.

And do you know what else? I never again denied Jesus the rest of my life! I was in prison, was beaten, suffered many things because of my preaching for Jesus, but I stuck by His side. That's how Jesus helped me grow.

Thank your storyteller. Then say, We all have times when we fail to do what we know is right. We lie, get angry, hurt others by our actions, sometimes we may even deny that we are Christians.

- Think of a time when you hurt someone. How did that make you feel? *(Allow students to respond.)*

- Is there a time when you failed to speak up and tell people you were a Christian? How did that make you feel? *(Allow students to respond.)*

- Think of a time when you wanted to do the right thing but did the wrong thing instead. How did you feel about that? *(Allow students to respond.)*

- There may be a time when you did something and found out later that it was the wrong thing to do. How did you feel then? *(Allow students to respond.)*

We all do wrong things because we are not spiritually grown up. We are still growing. But each day we live, we can grow stronger spiritually. In our Lesson Activity, we will find out how.

LESSON ACTIVITY: Spiritual Food Groups

 Before Class: Draw the following Food Pyramid chart on the chalkboard. Leave plenty of room to write foods under each group.

THE FOOD PYRAMID

1. Fats, oils, sweets *(use sparingly)*

2. Milk, yogurt, and cheese group *(2–3 servings)*

3. Meat, poultry, fish, dry beans, eggs, and nuts group *(2–3 servings)*

4. Vegetable and fruit group *(Vegetables: 3–5 servings)* *(Fruits: 2–4 servings)*

5. Bread, cereal, rice, and pasta group *(6–11 servings)*

Pass out the food labels you brought. Direct the students' attention to The Food Pyramid. Let's look at this pyramid and see the foods that we need to eat every day. **Read through the chart.** These foods are important because they contain vitamins and minerals and other nutrients to keep our bodies healthy and to help them grow. I'm sure you've learned about these five food groups in school.

Look at the labels I gave you. Let's see which foods are represented in the food chart and the vitamins and minerals each food provides. **Have each student name the food on each of his labels, the main two vitamins or minerals found in that food, and which group the food belongs to. Write the name of the food under the correct group.**

We also have five "spiritual food" groups. As we make sure we get some of each group in our life, we will grow strong and healthy spiritually.

On another part of the chalkboard, write this chart.

> ### THE FIVE SPIRITUAL GROWTH GROUPS
>
> *1. We must study God's Word.*
>
> *2. We must pray.*
>
> *3. We must fellowship with other Christians.*
>
> *4. We must witness for Christ.*
>
> *5. We must obey God.*

Unlike The Food Pyramid, the Five Spiritual Growth Groups don't have a recommended number of servings per day. Some are not more important than others. They are all equally important.

Read through each group, discussing when each should be practiced. Bring out the following suggestions.

1. We must study God's Word—*(A Christian should read God's Word every day.)*

2. We must pray—*(We should pray all the time—every chance we get. Sometimes our prayers should be aloud and other times they can be silently in our hearts.)*

3. We must fellowship with other Christians—*(We should go to church every week to be with the people of God. Throughout the week, we should spend time with Christian friends.)*

4. We must witness for Christ—*(Each day as we have an opportunity, we should tell others about Jesus and how much He loves them.)*

5. We must obey God—*(Obedience should be a part of every moment of our day.)*

• Why do you think each Spiritual Growth Group is important for our spiritual growth?
   (Studying the Bible helps us know what God wants us to do, so we can do what's right.)

(When we pray we talk to God and that's important. Then God helps us grow.)

(Having Christian friends and going to church will help us do the right things and make good choices.)

(Telling other people about Jesus will help them start growing too. Telling other people about Jesus helps us remember how much He loves us.)

(Obeying God is important for all the rest of the Spiritual Growth Groups. If I don't obey God, I won't become a grown-up Christian.)

- Which one of the five groups is probably the hardest for you to do?

    (Studying God's Word because I am not a good reader. I don't know how to study the Bible.)

    (Praying because I don't know how. I forget to pray.)

    (Going to church because I like to sleep in on Sundays. Getting together with Christian friends because there aren't any in my neighborhood.)

    (Telling other people about Jesus because I'm scared they will make fun of me.)

    (Obeying God because sometimes I do wrong things. Sometimes I forget to obey God.)

CHECK FOR UNDERSTANDING: Check It Out!

It's important to do all five of the Spiritual Growth Groups so we can grow well. Let's see if you can recognize all five of the principles of Christian growth that we learned.

Distribute the "Spiritual Growth Groups" handouts and pencils. Have students write the correct principle under each diagram.

APPLICATION: Growing Up Strong

Now that we know about The Food Pyramid and the Five Spiritual Growth Groups, let's see how well we're doing in both areas. **Make sure students have pencils.** On the back of your handout, write down everything you ate in the last 24 hours. Don't forget to include candy, soda, and chips. Jot down what you ate at each meal and any in-between snacks. **Give students time to think and write.**

Now put the number of the food group beside each food you ate. Did you have enough servings of each group? Check it out. **Give students time to think and write. Then briefly discuss which food groups are least represented in what the students ate.**

Now let's do the same for the Five Spiritual Growth Groups. Write the numbers 1 through 5 on the back of your handout. As I ask each question, write your answer next to each number.

1. In the past week, how many times have you read the Bible?

2. In the last 24 hours, how many times have you talked to God?

3. In the past week, how much time have you spent with Christian friends? How much time have you spent in church?

4. In the past week, how many people did you tell about Jesus?

5. In the last 24 hours, how many things did you do that you know for sure were disobedient to God?

The point is not to keep absolute track of everything you do, like you might do with The Food Pyramid. Instead, these questions should help you see which Groups are the most difficult for you. With The Food Pyramid, you could adopt a diet that contains food from all the groups. As you grow older, the specific foods you like will change, but you should always try to eat something from each of the groups. In the same way, you will be doing the Spiritual Growth Groups all your life. As you grow spiritually, you will find new ways of doing them. A more grown-up Christian will have a different plan for spiritual growth than you will. The important point is to be aware of the groups and have a plan to make sure they all have an important place in your life.

On your "Spiritual Growth Groups" worksheet is a plan. Take a few minutes right now to fill it out. **Give students time to think and write. Put aside the worksheets until you close the class.**

MEMORY VERSE ACTIVITY: Memory Mix Up!

2 Timothy 2:15—"Do your best to present yourself to God as one approved, a workman who does not need to be ashamed and who correctly handles the word of truth."

> *Before Class:* Write each word of the memory verse on 30 squares of construction paper, mixing up the letters. For example, "Do" would be "oD" or "present" could be "tpeenrs." Place "2 Timothy" on one square and "2:15" on another. Make two sets of squares, using a different color for each set. Write the memory verse on the chalkboard.

Divide students into two teams and assign each team the color of one set of squares. Have each team sit in a circle on the floor.

Read the memory verse to the students. A worker in God's kingdom works hard to study the Bible and do what it says. Our memory verse tells us this fact when it says that he or she "handles the word of truth." Learning the Bible is one way a Christian grows. To learn our memory verse for today, we'll first figure out the mixed-up words that spell our memory verse. Then we'll place the words in order.

Put one set of mixed-up words in the center of each circle. When you say "Go," each team will unscramble the words and put them in order to complete the verse. The first team to put their words in order will stand and say the verse aloud. Do this activity two or three times. Then erase the words on the chalkboard and see if the teams can put the words in order without help. Allow individuals to recite the verse.

WEEKLY ASSIGNMENT: A Great Plan

Have students take out their "Spiritual Growth Groups" worksheets. This week, use the plan you made earlier to help you continue to grow spiritually. If you practice what you wrote on your worksheet for a few weeks, you will soon make a habit of doing the Spiritual Growth Groups. Put your plan in a place where you can see it often—perhaps in your bedroom or on the refrigerator. Tell one Christian friend about your plan and ask that friend to remind you to do it. We will discuss how your plan worked during our next class.

Spiritual Growth Groups

Write the correct Spiritual Growth Group under each diagram.

 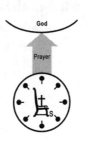 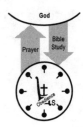

1._____ 2._____ 5._____

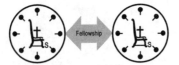 

3._____ 4._____

My Plan for Using the Spiritual Growth Groups

GROUP 1:

I will study my Bible once a week on this day: _____

I will read my Bible every day at this time: _____

GROUP 2: I will pray three times a day at these times: _____

_____

GROUP 3: I will go to church at these times: _____

I will ask this Christian friend to help me remember to practice this Growth Plan:

_____

GROUP 4: I will tell this person about Jesus: _____

GROUP 5: I will obey God in each area of my Growth Plan for the next week.

Signed: _____

Critical Communication

LESSON PLAN

OBJECTIVE: Students will learn the importance of studying the Bible and praying.

APPLICATION: Students will develop a plan to study the Bible and to have a regular time of prayer.

LESSON PLAN ELEMENT	ACTIVITY	TIME	SUPPLIES
Opening Activity	*Listening Ears*	7–10	Blindfold; flashlight; pillowcase or towel
Bible Story—Psalm 119:105; Philippians 4:6, two principles of growth	*What Should I Do?*	10–15	Bible; "My Communication with God" notebooks; pencils
Lesson Activity	*Bible Study Matching Game*	7–10	Bibles; yellow, red, blue, and green construction paper; 1 copy of the "Bible Study Matching Game" handout; scissors; glue; notebooks; pencils
Application	*Constant Communication*	7–10	Notebooks; pencils
Check for Understanding	*Flash-Card Principles*	3–5	"Spiritual Growth Groups" handout from Lesson 7; glue; scissors; large cards
Memory Verse Activity	*Pass the Pad*	3–5	Pad, pencil; audiocassette player; music tape
Weekly Assignment	*Keep It Up!*	3–5	Notebooks; "Keep It Up!" handouts; pencils; tape

Communication is a vital element in any successful relationship, including our relationship with God. In our spiritual walk, we have two avenues of communication with God that are essential to our spiritual growth. We learned about these principles in the previous lesson: learning what God has to say to us through Bible study (*We must study God's Word*) and talking with God through prayer (*We must pray*).

These two spiritual growth principles form the basis of our Christian life. God desires that we study His Word to learn more about Him, His standards for us, and His love for people. He also wants us to communicate with Him about our cares and concerns. He desires that we talk to Him about every area of our lives. This communication with God is called prayer. These two areas of communication are our vertical relationship. (Another area of communication is our horizontal relationship, or our relationship with other believers and the church.)

God's Word, which is divinely inspired, is the basis of our belief as Christians. It gives us God's perspective on how we should live and how we can be fruitful witnesses for our Lord Jesus Christ. The Bible is God's love letter to man. From Genesis to Revelation, it tells of God's great compassion for us and of His desire to fellowship with us.

If elementary students learn how to dig into God's Word at their early age, they will have a better opportunity to grow and develop spiritually as they mature into adults. As your students apply God's truth to their lives and learn more about His character, they can avoid the problems that afflict so many believers who did not have the advantage of early spiritual training.

Learning to pray is also essential for spiritual growth. Prayer is much more than words. It is an expression of the heart toward God. It is an experience, a relationship—not merely an activity.

As children of God, we are invited to come boldly before His throne (Hebrews 4:14–16). Because the One to whom we pray is the King of kings and Lord of lords, the Creator of heaven and earth, we come into His presence with reverence. But He is also our loving heavenly Father who cares for us. Therefore, we can enter into His presence with a relaxed, joyful heart, knowing that God loves us more than anyone else has ever loved us or ever will love us.

Your students can find comfort, peace, and strength in developing an active prayer routine. Many young people face problems far greater than those you faced at their age. They are confronted with ideologies that conflict with a biblical viewpoint. They need to be assured that their heavenly Father is intimately concerned with their well-being and that He listens to His children. Having a vital prayer life where requests are answered and thanksgiving is nurtured can give them that assurance during tough times.

This lesson prepares students for extended Bible study and prayer. To help them, purchase small notebooks to give to them. On the front of each notebook, write "My Communication with God."

LESSON PLAN

OPENING ACTIVITY: Listening Ears

Discuss the problems and successes of using the chart "My Plan for Using the Spiritual Growth Groups." Compliment students who tried hard to implement all five growth areas. Encourage students to keep using the growth principles consistently.

Ask a student or an adult to role-play a situation with you where someone is talking to another person who isn't listening.

 Optional Activity: Have your students cover one ear and compare to what they can hear with both ears.

- What was happening in that scene? *(That person wasn't listening to you. That person was being rude.)*

- Have you ever been in a situation like this? How did it make you feel? *(Allow students to describe situations and how they felt.)*

Maybe you've tried to talk to a friend who was watching TV. Or you may have told your mom to pick you up at 4:30 but she didn't show up because she wasn't listening. Maybe in school the teacher was talking and asked you a question, but you couldn't answer because you weren't listening. To help us think about the importance of listening, we are going to play a game.

Have the students sit in chairs forming a large circle. Write these three categories on the board: "Hit," "Close miss," and "Miss." Blindfold one student and have him or her sit in the middle holding a flashlight.

As you silently point to one student sitting in the circle, have the student clap once. The blindfolded student will then point the flashlight in the direction from which the sound came. If the beam lands on the student who clapped, it's a hit. If the beam lands on the student on either side, it's a close miss. Anywhere else is a miss. Let the blindfolded student try 2 or 3 times. Use tally marks to record the results on the board. Then let another student have a turn in the center. When everyone has had a turn, reassemble and discuss the results.

- What was the hardest thing for you in the game? *(Locating the exact spot of the sound; being able to hear correctly.)*

Listening clearly takes a lot of concentration and work. That's true for us with everyday things too. Everything we do requires listening.

- Who is the most important person to listen to? *(God.)*

- What are some ways we can listen to God? *(Through Bible study and prayer.)*

God wants us to listen to Him and follow His direction for our lives. How does God talk to us? He talks to us through His Word the Bible. We talk with Him through prayer.

Let's listen to some real-life situations to help us understand how to better communicate with God.

BIBLE STORY: What Should I Do?

These stories present difficult problems, which may be similar to some your students face. Do not try to come up with answers to solve the problems. Your students do not have the maturity or wisdom to handle problems like these on their own. What they need to know is where to go to get support. Distribute the notebooks and pencils to your students. Explain that these notebooks will record their private conversations with God.

I'm going to tell you two stories. In one story, the main character is a girl who is having difficulties. After I finish the story, we'll discuss what the girl could do to help her problem. Then I'll tell a story about a boy. We'll discuss what the boy could do to help his problem.

But before we begin, I'm going to read two Bible verses. As I tell the stories, think about these verses. Then use what the verses say to help you discuss the answers. **Have students write the principle of growth and the verse references in their notebooks as you read. You may want to write this information on the chalkboard.**

1   We must study God's Word (Psalm 119:105). **Read verse.**

2.   We must pray (Philippians 4:6). **Read verse.**

Jasmine lived in a family where she had a fifteen-year-old brother named Jeremy, her mother, and her stepfather, George. Jeremy and George didn't get along at all. Jeremy was always doing something to make him mad, and then her stepfather would "blow his top." Jasmine secretly thought that Jeremy liked to watch George get mad.

Jasmine hated those scenes. What made it worse was that Jeremy would often find a way to drag her into the middle of the fight.

Several months ago, Jasmine started going to church with her best friend, Amanda. Jasmine noticed that Amanda's family hardly ever had big fights like those at her house. Most of the time, Amanda's parents were able to work out any problems they had with their children, and the children listened to their parents when they were caught disobeying the family's rules. At church, Jasmine's Sunday school teacher was helping her learn how to study the Bible. Just two weeks ago, Jasmine learned how to become a Christian and asked Jesus to be her Savior. Now she wants to live like a Christian should. But that is sometimes hard for her to do.

Yesterday, when her mother was at work, Jeremy had a big argument with George. It all started when Jeremy came into the house smelling like cigarette smoke. He walked right by George who was sitting in the recliner reading his newspaper. Jeremy knew that his stepfather was totally against smoking. In fact, George's father had died of lung cancer just a few years ago. Jasmine knew Jeremy walked by George just to make him mad.

BEGINNING THE CHRISTIAN ADVENTURE

George said in an angry voice, "I can smell cigarette smoke on you. That's the second time I've caught you smoking."

Jeremy had a smirk on his face. "So what? And if I do, what's it to you?"

George's face began to get red. That always meant trouble. Jasmine wanted to escape from the living room, but couldn't get past Jeremy and George to the doorway.

George started yelling about how he knew what was good for Jeremy and that Jeremy was turning into a troublemaker. Jasmine started inching her way to the door when Jeremy turned to her. "I don't have to listen to George," he said. "He's not my dad. I don't need a father and I don't want one! Right, Jasmine?"

Jasmine always sided with Jeremy at this point because she didn't like George telling them what to do either. George always left his stuff around the house and she had to pick it all up. He never complimented anyone and always had his eyes tuned to the TV or hidden behind a newspaper. So she said, "Mom's the boss around here as far as I'm concerned. She's the only one who can tell me what to do."

That made the fight even worse. George got angrier and shouted even louder. The fight ended when Jeremy walked out of the house.

- What was Jasmine's problem in this story? (*She didn't want to be in the middle of the fight. She didn't like her stepfather. Jeremy always got her involved in his fights.*)

- Jasmine can't solve her problem alone. Where could she find help? (*She could talk to her Sunday school teacher. She could find answers in the Bible. She could talk to Amanda's parents. She could talk to her mother.*)

- If you were Amanda, what could you do to help your friend who is a new Christian? (*I could tell her to talk to my parents. I could pray with her and help her learn how to talk to God. I could show her how the Bible tells us to obey those in charge of us.*)

If Jasmine studied the Bible, she would learn what God says about listening to those who are in charge. She could ask other Christians to help her find out what God says.

Our second story takes place at school. Ryan comes from a poor family. He never wears designer jeans or has the right kind of athletic shoes. He tried out for the soccer team, but his parents couldn't buy him the gear, so he had to quit.

Ryan has no friends at school. Many of the kids call him "Loser." He thinks that nickname is true of him. He has trouble remembering spelling words, gets his math facts mixed up, and can't write a good sentence. Sometimes he just puts down any answer on his tests because he knows he won't get anything right anyway.

Many times, Ryan gets in trouble at recess for fighting with other boys. He never starts the fights, but there are three boys in his class who pick on him. Because he gets into trouble so often, the yard-duty person is quick to give him detention. So he's often either going on detention or just getting off. When the principal asked his parents to come to school for a conference about his fighting, his parents didn't show up.

Last month, a new boy named Chris entered his class. Chris was kind of shy and didn't make friends easily. For some reason, Chris liked Ryan. They began playing together at recess.

Chris told Ryan that Jesus loves him. Ryan had never heard anything like that before. He went to the boys' club at Ryan's church and heard all about how God loves everyone. Ryan became a Christian and began reading his Bible.

One day, one of the boys who always picked on Ryan brought a pocketknife to school. He let Ryan put it in his pocket. Ryan felt so important. But he knew about the school's "no tolerance" rule for weapons. He knew what he was doing was wrong.

Someone told the teacher that Ryan had a knife in his pocket. Ryan was suspended for three days. His parents were very mad!

- What was Ryan's problem? *(He didn't obey the school's rules. He didn't have many friends. He had a hard time in school.)*

- Ryan can't solve his problems alone. Where could he go for help? *(He could ask his boys' club leader to help him. He could ask Chris to help. He could learn what to do by reading God's Word.)*

- If you were Chris, what could you do to help Ryan? *(I could still be his friend even though he got suspended. I could tell him to talk to someone at church who could help him. I could help him with his homework so he wouldn't feel so dumb. I could help him study the Bible to learn how to be more like Jesus.)*

The Bible tells us about different ways we can get help with our problems. We are never alone. God will help us. We can listen to what He says to us by studying the Bible. Christian friends can help us learn what is in the Bible, too. In our Lesson Activity, we will find out what we can do to grow spiritually so we can live the way we should.

LESSON ACTIVITY: Bible Study Matching Game

Before Class: Make the cards for the "Bible Study Matching Game." Cut 15 3"×3" cards from yellow construction paper. Photocopy the "Bible Study Matching Game" reproducible and cut out the statements. Glue them onto the yellow 3"×3" cards. Then cut 5 red 3"×3" cards. Write on each "What are the facts?" Cut 5 blue 3"×3" cards and write on each "What do the facts mean?" Cut 5 green 3"×3" cards and write on each "What does God want me to do?" The game works best if you have no more than 10 students. If there are more than that in your class, make two sets of cards and play two games at once.

Teaching Tip: The three categories in the "Bible Study Matching Game" correspond to a basic Bible study method with three steps. "What are the facts?" corresponds to the "observation" step. "What do the facts mean?" corresponds to the "interpretation" step. And "What does God want me to do?" corresponds to the "application" step. By playing this game, your students will be introduced to this simple Bible study method. For more practice, select another easy Bible story and write 5 observation, 5 interpretation, and 5 application sentences on colored cards. Suggested Scripture passages are Ruth 1:1–19 and Acts 12:1–16.

If you remember, in our last lesson we studied the five Spiritual Growth Groups: *We must study God's Word. We must pray. We must fellowship with other Christians. We must witness for Christ. We must obey God.* Three of these are communication principles. When we study God's Word, He speaks to us through the Bible. And when we pray, we speak to Him. When we fellowship with other Christians, we talk to each other to help and support each other. Just like we learned in the Opening Activity, we need to listen to God when we communicate with Him.

For this activity, we are going to discuss one of the communication principles of spiritual growth: *We must study God's Word.* Later, we will learn more about *We must pray.*

Have students form pairs and read Daniel 6:1–23 with their partners. Circulate and help students with words that may be difficult.

When they finish reading, have each pair work as a team in the "Bible Study Matching Game." Have students form a circle with their partner beside them. Place the pile of yellow cards face down in the middle. Put the other three colors in separate piles facing up so you can read them. The first pair draws one card from the yellow pile and reads the card aloud. The pair decides which of the other three types of cards matches their card, and then draws that card. If they are correct, they keep both cards. If they are incorrect, they put each card at the bottom of the appropriate piles. The next pair then draws a yellow card. The play continues around the circle until all cards are gone. The pair with the most cards wins. Applaud the winner.

The game we played helped us learn a way to study the Bible. You can use this same method to study any part of the Bible. Just follow these easy steps. **Write these steps on the chalkboard. Instruct students to write the steps in their notebooks under the heading "Steps for Bible Study."**

1. Read the Bible verses.

   Then you can use your notebook to record your answers to these questions:

2. What are the facts?

3. What do the facts mean?

4. What does God want me to do?

Once you have studied the Bible passage, you will usually find one or two things that God is telling you to do.

- How does it make you feel to know that God wants you to study His Word on your own? *(Scared because I'm not a good reader. Excited, because I think I'm old enough to do that. Worried, because I don't think I'll do a good enough job.)*

Studying God's Word is important for all Christians to do. You don't have to be an adult to do it. If you have problems reading, you can get a Bible that uses simple language. Of course, we all need to check what we think about the Bible with more mature Christians who have studied the Bible for a long time. But God wants to speak to you through His Word and He wants you to study it for yourself too. As you study, you will get better at it and it will become more exciting. But the important part of studying God's Word is doing what it says. That's called applying it to your life.

- What was one thing that our Daniel passage told us to do? *(Pray three times a day. Pray even when it's hard. Stick up for what's right even when other people don't want you to.)*

- How do you think God wants you to apply the facts you learned in this passage to your own life? *(Allow students to apply these verses to their own situations. If they have problems, suggest ways they could pray. Emphasize the principle that we should pray even when others make fun of us for doing it.)*

Now let's go on to the other growth principle we learned, *We must pray.* We can do certain things to help us pray more effectively.

APPLICATION: Constant Communication

- If you were explaining prayer to a person who had never prayed before, what would you say? *(Prayer is talking to God. Prayer is telling God about everything, even our sins.)*

Let's look at some promises God gives us about prayer. **Divide the class into three groups. Give each group two of the following references. Have groups look up the verses and write in their notebooks a promise that God gives us about prayer. Then have groups report to the class about their passages.**

Philippians 4:6—*(We can talk to God about anything.)*

Matthew 26:41—*(Prayer can keep us from sin.)*

Matthew 6:6—*(God will reward our prayers.)*

Matthew 18:20—*(When we pray with others, God will be there.)*

Luke 11:9–13—*(God will give us good things when we ask Him.)*

John 14:13,14—*(Jesus will answer our prayers when we ask in His name.)*

All day long, we can have constant communication with God. We can pray anywhere, at any time. There are four simple steps to prayer. On a clean page in your notebook, write "Steps to Prayer." Under the heading, write these steps and the Bible verse references as I give them. Underline the first word in each step to help you remember it. **Write these on the board as you give them.**

1. Live every day in Jesus—John 15:7. **Read verse.**

2. Ask God for what you need—James 4:2,3. **Read verses.**

3. Believe that God will answer—Matthew 21:22. **Read verse.**

4. Receive the answer to your prayer—1 John 5:14,15. **Read verses.**

Every time you pray, you tap into the greatest power in the world—God's power. You also tap into His love and His wisdom. God can do great and mighty things through you when you pray.

Of course, when we pray, we must always want God's way first. We must listen to God. Our prayers must not be selfish. God knows what's best for us and He will answer with the best gift for us. Therefore, we must be patient and allow God to do the best thing for our situation.

We also must pray for each other. That's how *We must fellowship with other Christians* fits into our prayer. We pray for our Christian friends and we pray with them. When we pray, we must always pray according to God's will. We find His will in the Bible. That's how *We must study God's Word* fits into our prayer. We cannot get answers to prayers that go against what God says in His Word. When we ask God to do what His Word says, we are practicing *We must obey God*. When we tell other people about how good God is and how they can know God too, that's how we practice the principle, *We must witness for Christ.*

Divide students into pairs. Have one partner mention a prayer request to the other partner. Have partners discuss how the request would be in line with God's Word. (Circulate and help pairs with this part of their request.) Then have partners take time to pray for the request. Reverse roles and have partners pray again. Encourage students to write their partner's prayer request in their notebooks for later prayer.

CHECK FOR UNDERSTANDING: Flash-Card Principles

Photocopy the five diagrams from the Lesson Introduction for Lesson 7. Cut them apart and mount them on cards to make flash cards.

Remind students of the five Spiritual Growth Groups: We must study God's Word; We must pray; We must fellowship with other Christians; We must witness for Christ; We must obey God. Then hold up the flash cards to see if your group can answer quickly. Go through the cards several times.

MEMORY VERSE ACTIVITY: Pass the Pad

1 Thessalonians 2:13—"We also thank God continually because, when you received the word of God, which you heard from us, you accepted it not as the word of men, but as it actually is, the word of God, which is at work in you who believe."

Write the verse on the board or on a poster.

Read 1 Thessalonians 2:13 to the students. Have the students read it to you. This verse is telling us that we should study God's Word because it helps us know the truth. Just as we talked about today, God wants us to spend time reading the Bible and praying to Him.

Have the students repeat the verse together several times. Then have them sit in a circle. Play music while the students pass a pad and pencil around the circle. Periodically stop the music. Begin reading the verse but stop partway. Have the student holding the pad and pencil write the next word in the verse. If the word is correct, he or she stays in the circle. If it isn't correct, the student comes out of the circle for that turn and reads the verse part you have chosen when the music stops.

After doing this several times, make the game more difficult by having the students write the first word of the verse when the music stops, then the second word on the next turn until the whole verse has been written down. When the verse has been completed, have the class repeat the whole verse together.

WEEKLY ASSIGNMENT: Keep It Up!
Distribute the "Keep It Up!" handouts.

Tape your handout inside the cover of your notebook. Write the answers to the questions on a page in your notebook. This week, use your notebook every day. For each day, follow the instructions on the worksheet. You will be studying the Bible and praying each day. For your Bible study, read John chapter 11. It will probably take you a whole week to go through this chapter. Take your time and do a good job. **Have students write "John 11" on the first blank line on their handouts.**

Close in prayer, asking God to help your students develop good Bible study and prayer habits.

> *Teaching Tip:* This lesson is particularly important for your students' spiritual growth. You may want to help your students keep using their notebooks for the next five lessons to help them develop a habit of Bible study and prayer. If you do, set aside a few moments at the beginning of each lesson to examine their notebooks and discuss the passage studied and its application. When students complete one passage, assign another one. Some students may be able to work through a book such as the Gospel of Mark or John. Encourage students to ask any questions they have. Emphasize that no one has all the answers to every question about the Bible but that many questions will be answered as they grow and mature in Christ.

Bible Study Matching Game

Photocopy this page and cut out the 15 statements. Note which statements are in which category so you can identify them during the game. Glue the statements onto yellow 3"×3" cards.

What are the facts? (observation)	What do the facts mean? (interpretation)	What does God want me to do? (application)
The king made a law that no one could pray to God.	Although the king made a law against praying, Daniel knew he must still talk to God and that he would be disobeying God if he didn't pray.	Even when it is difficult to do so, I will pray at least three times a day.
Daniel prayed to God although he knew he could lose his life if he prayed.	Daniel knew he could trust God—whether he was saved from the lions or not.	Because I see how God protected Daniel in his troubles, I will trust God in my troubles too.
The king's law said that anyone who prayed to God would be thrown into the hungry lions' den.	God is able to do anything—even close the mouths of hungry lions. God is stronger than the king and the administrators.	Daniel didn't know if God would save him from the lions, but he prayed anyway. I will obey God even though I don't know how God will work out my situation.
Daniel was caught praying and thrown into the lions' den.	Daniel prayed three times a day like he always did because he knew how important it is to talk to God.	Daniel stayed true to God even though others tried to stop him. I will stay true to God no matter what my friends think.
God protected Daniel in the lions' den.	The administrators in the kingdom wanted to trap Daniel and have him killed because they were jealous of him.	Daniel told the king that God had saved him from the lions. I will tell others how God answers my prayers.

Keep It Up!

Bible passage I will study: _____

What are the facts?

What do the facts mean?

What does God want me to do?

Time and place I will pray:

    Time _____

    Place _____

People I will pray for:

Things I will ask God for:

Things I will praise and thank God for:

Passport to a Joyful Life

BOOK OBJECTIVE	To introduce students to Jesus and the Christian life and to help them begin to grow as believers.
UNIT OBJECTIVE	To help students begin growing in their relationship with Christ by producing godly fruit, confessing their sins, and preparing for spiritual battle.
LESSON 9: New Creatures	*Objective:* To help students understand their new life in Christ and how to begin growing. *Application:* To help students list two changes they would like to make in their life.
LESSON 10: Digging Up the Dirt	*Objective:* To help students evaluate their relationship with God through learning about the parable of the soil and seeds. *Application:* To help students decide on three ways to produce fruit in their lives and how to implement them at home.
LESSON 11: Wipe It Clean!	*Objective:* To help students learn the importance of living the cleansed life moment by moment. *Application:* To help students make a record of the wrongs they have committed, confess these sins to God, and destroy the list to signify God's forgiveness.
LESSON 12: The Great Battle	*Objective:* To help students learn about spiritual warfare and how to use the armor God has provided for the battle. *Application:* To help students identify one personal problem situation and an appropriate piece of armor to use in that situation.
LESSON 13: Passport to Adventure	*Objective:* To help students review the concept of living the abundant life in Christ. *Application:* To help students learn how to continue progressing in their Christian adventure.

The Christian life is one of purpose, victory, joy, and peace. Jesus said, "The thief comes only to steal and kill and destroy; I have come that they may have life, and have it to the full" (John 10:10).

Although many professing Christians are living in defeat and discouragement, this is not the New Testament norm. Picture the apostle Paul and Silas imprisoned in Philippi. They were beaten and cast into prison where their feet were locked in the stocks. Yet they prayed and sang praises to God. Their confidence was not in themselves. Their trust was in the true living God whom they loved, worshiped, and served.

Picture, too, the disciples and thousands of other first-century Christians singing praises to God as they were burned at the stake, crucified, or fed to the lions. They faced horrible deaths with courage and joy because of their vital, personal relationship with Jesus.

Down through the centuries, there have been—and still are—hundreds of millions of Christians who have dedicated their very lives to Christ and have enjoyed the abundant life Christ promised. Many have seen friends and relatives for whom they prayed invite Jesus to be Savior and Lord. Others have overcome destructive habits and attitudes to experience joy and confidence.

This unit will introduce your students to the abundant life they are entitled to as followers of Jesus. Most preteens are anxious to try the more daring and unusual experiences in life. As they grow through the teen years, they will have an even greater desire to taste life at its fullest.

As Christian teachers, we have the privilege of introducing students to a life filled with excitement, joy, and eternal benefits. We can divert our students' interests away from the dark world of drugs, illicit sex, and pornography into a relationship with Christ which is much more satisfying than any other activity or relationship.

This unit will help equip your students with practical ways they can apply what they have learned about walking in faith. They will decide which areas are out of control in their lives and plan ways to turn these problems over to Christ. Students will also learn ways to fight temptation in their lives. The last lesson is a review of the entire book. It also will challenge your students to continue with what they have learned.

If you plan to go on to the next book in this series, you will be discovering more about who God is and what He has done for us. Book 2 of the Children's Discipleship Series, *Discovering Our Awesome God,* includes units on who God is, who the Holy Spirit is, and how to talk to God. This is the next step in your students' adventure with God.

New Creatures

LESSON PLAN

OBJECTIVE: Students will understand their new life in Christ and how to begin growing.

APPLICATION: Students will list two changes they would like to make in their lives.

LESSON PLAN ELEMENT	ACTIVITY	TIME	SUPPLIES
Opening Activity	*Changing Creatures*	7–10	"New Creatures" handouts; colored markers (optional)
Bible Story—Colossians 1:13,14, going from Satan's kingdom to God's kingdom	*Living in a New Kingdom*	10–15	Bibles
Lesson Activity	*Old to New*	7–10	White board and dry-erase marker; magazines; scissors; tape or sticky tac
Check for Understanding	*Attitude Counts*	3–5	Bible
Application	*Colorful Changes*	8–12	Unlined 3"×5"cards; scissors; glue; paper punch; fine-tip markers or pens; scraps of various colors of construction paper; "New Creatures" handouts
Memory Verse Activity	*Old Nature/New Nature*	2–3	
Weekly Assignment	*Butterfly Beginning*	3–5	Butterfly cards from Application

The Christian life begins with receiving the Lord Jesus Christ—the gift of God's love and forgiveness—by faith. It involves a threefold commitment to the Lord Jesus Christ: a commitment of your intellect, emotions, and will.

The Christian life is a personal, intimate relationship between you and Christ. This life begins in faith (Ephesians 2:8,9) and can only be lived by faith. Faith is another word for trust. We trust our lives to Christ's keeping because He has proven Himself trustworthy by His life, His death, His resurrection, and His abiding presence—His unconditional love.

As you walk in faith and obedience to God as an act of your will and allow Him to change your life, you will gain increasing assurance of your relationship with Him. You will experience God's work in your life as He enables you to do what you cannot do on your own.

Many religions, however, teach that starting over in life means revamping yourself and doing better. This is against what God teaches in His Word. He says that we are full of sin and unable to do a "make over" on our own.

When the Holy Spirit comes into our lives, He doesn't just redo what is already there. He gives us a totally new nature—His nature. We have His power, strength, and wisdom flowing through our new nature.

This old nature/new nature concept is important for your students to understand. They will always fail—as we all will—if they try to rely on their own efforts to transform their lives. Instead, they must realize that God is all-sufficient and we are dependent on Him for our spiritual life.

The change of a caterpillar to a butterfly is such a beautiful picture of what happens when we receive Jesus as our Savior. Although we are the same creature—created by God with value and purpose—He gives us a new nature so that we can fulfill what He intended us to be. Encourage your students to thank God for their new nature.

LESSON PLAN

OPENING ACTIVITY: Changing Creatures

 Before Class: When you photocopy the "New Creatures" master, copy the information page on the back of the drawings page.

Distribute the "New Creatures" handouts. If you want students to color the insect drawings, have them do so as you discuss each picture.

Let me read the verse we are going to talk about in this lesson. **Read 2 Corinthians 5:17.**

- What does this verse say happened to you when you received Christ? *(Christians become new creatures or creations. Our old life is gone now.)*

To help us understand more about what this verse is saying, let me show you some of God's creatures that make a change for the better. **Point out the caterpillar picture.** This is a caterpillar.

- Can anyone tell me what the caterpillar will change into? *(A butterfly.)*

Point out the picture of the butterfly.

- What makes this butterfly better than its old self, the caterpillar? *(It is more beautiful. It can fly to get around. It is bigger and able to protect itself more.)*

- Is this butterfly a completely different creature than the caterpillar? *(No.)*

The butterfly is still the caterpillar, but it has changed into a new kind of creature. It has many more features than the caterpillar. **Read the butterfly facts on the handout.**

Point out the picture of the maggot.

- Can anyone tell me what this maggot will change into? *(A housefly.)*

- What makes this housefly better than its maggot stage? *(It's able to fly. It can protect itself better. It can go places it couldn't go before.)*

- Is this housefly a completely different creature than the maggot? *(No.)*

The housefly is still the same creature as the maggot, but it has changed into a new form. It has many more features than the maggot. **Read the housefly facts.**

Point out the nymph stage of the mosquito.

- Can anyone tell me what this creature will turn into? *(A mosquito.)*

Point out the picture of the mosquito.

- What makes this mosquito better than its nymph stage? *(It's able to fly. It can protect itself better. It can bite people to get food.)*

- Is this mosquito a completely different creature than the nymph? *(No.)*

This is still the nymph but it has changed into a mosquito. It has many more features than the nymph. **Read the mosquito facts.**

The changes these insects make can show us what happens to us when we ask Christ to come into our lives. The Bible calls it a second birth. We become a new "spiritual" creation in Christ. You are the same person, but God gives you a new nature, a spiritual nature that can obey Him.

During our Bible story, we will learn more about what happens to us when we become a new creation in Christ.

BIBLE STORY: Living in a New Kingdom

Divide your room into two parts, one with dim lighting to represent Satan's dark kingdom and the other with bright lighting to represent Christ's kingdom of light. Begin the story time by having your students sit in the dimly lighted part of the room.

When you see a caterpillar crawling on the ground or on a leaf, you know that its world is very small. It can go only as far as it can crawl. It cannot run, hop, or fly. Can you imagine what it would be like to be a caterpillar and be so limited in where you can go?

But then the caterpillar forms a cocoon around itself. From looking at the caterpillar in its cocoon, you wouldn't know that anything was happening. The cocoon covers up what is going on inside.

Soon, the caterpillar breaks open the cocoon and emerges. It has wings—beautiful, colorful wings! It beats its wings until they are strong enough to fly.

- If you had changed from a caterpillar into a butterfly, what do you imagine you'd be thinking when you emerged from your cocoon? *(I would be surprised that I had wings. I'd think that flying would be so much fun.)*

- How is changing from a caterpillar to a butterfly similar to changing from a person who doesn't know Jesus to one who knows Him? *(We do different things that are more like what Jesus wants us to do. We think differently.)*

Now the butterfly has a whole new world to explore. It can flit around from flower to flower. It can travel to places it could not even see before. It can soar on the breezes. The colors on its wings are gorgeous.

We could say that the caterpillar lived in one kind of kingdom whereas the butterfly lives in another kind of kingdom. The caterpillar's kingdom is small and boring. The butterfly's kingdom is large and exciting.

This is what has happened to us. When we received Jesus as our Savior, we went from one kingdom to another—from Satan's kingdom to God's kingdom. **Read Colossians 1:13,14.** Our old kingdom was Satan's kingdom of darkness. Our new kingdom belongs to Jesus.

The caterpillar couldn't exist in the butterfly's kingdom. The caterpillar would fall to the ground and starve to death if it tried to live like a butterfly. The butterfly wouldn't want to live in the caterpillar's kingdom! That's why God created the caterpillar to change into an entirely new form. He didn't just paste wings on the caterpillar. God made every part of the butterfly to fit the butterfly's new kingdom existence.

That's what happens when we become Christians. Some people think that when you become a Christian, you are the same person but you just do different things. That's like pasting wings on a caterpillar. It doesn't work. Instead, God gives us a new nature when we become His children. He doesn't try to fix up the old nature; He gives us a new nature that fits us to live in the kingdom of His Son, Jesus.

Do you see how dim the light is in this part of the room? When we're in Satan's kingdom, we can't see things clearly. We can't even think the right way.

- What do you think Satan's kingdom is like? *(It's full of evil things. It is a place where you can't find love or happiness.)*

- Why do you think people stay in Satan's kingdom? *(They don't know there's a better one. They don't know how to get out. They think God's kingdom is boring.)*

Pair students. Make sure each pair has a Bible. Look up John 8:44. Find several things that are true about people who are in Satan's kingdom. **Give pairs a few moments to read and discuss. Then have students give responses about what they found. Some answers are: being a child of the devil, murdering, and lying.**

Now look up 1 John 3:10. That book is close to the end of the Bible. With your partner, find more things that are true about those who are in Satan's kingdom. **Give pairs a few moments to read and discuss. Then have students give responses.** *(Some answers are: not doing what's right; not loving your brother.)*

We could read many more verses that show us what Satan's kingdom is like. But from these two, we already can see that it is not a fun place to be. Now let's talk about Christ's kingdom. It is a kingdom of light rather than darkness.

Move students to the area with good lighting. People who live in Christ's kingdom can see the difference between right and wrong, just like we can see better with good lighting. That's because the Holy Spirit who lives in believers helps them understand the difference between right and wrong.

When we enter Christ's kingdom, we have all kinds of advantages. With your partner, read John 1:12,13 and find one advantage we have. *(Suggested answers: we become children of God; we are born of God.)*

Now, with your partner, read 2 Peter 1:4 and find another advantage of being in Christ's kingdom. The word corruption means evil. *(Suggested answers: we have the promises of God; we can escape the world's evil.)*

- Now that you know a little more about Christ's kingdom, how is it different from Satan's kingdom? *(God has love in His kingdom. We can be happy there. We have our sins forgiven in God's kingdom. We can do what's right.)*

In our Lesson Activity, we will learn more about the changes that we make when we go from Satan's kingdom into God's kingdom.

LESSON ACTIVITY: Old to New

Create the following chart on a white board:

	OLD	NEW
PHYSICAL		
SPIRITUAL		

Divide students into groups of three or four. If you have a small class, have students work in pairs or alone. Give each group a pair of scissors. Ask a student to read 2 Corinthians 5:17.

As you heard in the story about the two kingdoms, when Christ comes into our life many things about us change. Some of the bad things that we enjoyed doing before are not fun anymore. We become interested in the things of God. Let's make a chart to help us understand this better. **Hand out magazines and scissors.**

In your group, find a picture in the magazine of something that you had when you were small, such as baby food or a tricycle. Then find an item that you would replace it with when you are grown up, such as a steak or a car. Cut out these pictures. **Give groups a few minutes to do this and then discuss these items as a class. Tape the pictures under "Old" and "New" in the "Physical" column.**

Now let's come up with things that you did in your old life before you became a Christian. Let me help you with the first one. Maybe some of you had a hard time with lying. Let's write that under "Old" in the "Spiritual" column.

- What would replace it in our new life? *(Telling the truth.)*

Write "telling the truth" under "New" in the "Spiritual" column. Let's see if you can think of some more things we could put in our columns. **Continue doing this until you feel that they understand the concept of becoming a new creation.**

- How do we make this change from the old to the new? *(God does it for us. We can't do it on our own.)*

- How does it make you feel to know that you don't have to do it on your own? *(Pretty good. I'm glad because I've tried before and couldn't change.)*

Remember that some of our old, bad habits don't change overnight, but they will change as you stay close to Jesus Christ and ask Him to help you do what's right.

CHECK FOR UNDERSTANDING: Attitude Counts

Being a new creature in Christ means that you also have a new attitude or motivation. These verses give the motivation we should have as new creatures in Christ's kingdom. **Read 2 Corinthians 5:14,15.** Our new motivation or attitude is to do everything because we love Jesus and are grateful that He died for us. In each of the following situations, tell me which attitude shows you love Jesus. **Read the statements and the "A" and "B" choices after each one. Allow students to choose the correct answer.**

- Talking to friends

    A. Listening first

    B. Being anxious to say what I want to say

- Helping my little brother clean his room

    A. Being mad because my mom made me do it

    B. Thanking God for my little brother as I work

- Getting a difficult assignment at school

    A. Asking a smart person in class to do the assignment for me

    B. Doing my best and asking for help if I get stuck

- Being threatened by a bully on my way home from school

    A. Calling the bully bad names and planning to get even

    B. Telling a responsible adult about the situation and praying for the bully

In every situation, just ask yourself: What should I do to show that I love Jesus? If you do everything to please Him, your attitude will always count for good.

APPLICATION: Colorful Changes

Set out paper punch, glue, construction paper scraps, scissors, and markers. Have students trace and cut out their butterfly patterns from their "New Creatures" handouts. Show students how to fold the butterfly wings on either side of the body. Also have students punch out dots from the scraps of construction paper and glue them to their butterflies. As they work, ask:

- What are some of the greatest changes you have seen in your life since you became a new creation in Christ Jesus? (*Less fighting with my sisters; respecting my parents more; less lying; I care more what happens to other people instead of just myself.*)

Although we have a new nature, we still have our old nature, too. It tries to get us to do what we know we shouldn't do. It's like a battle inside. Our new nature fights our old nature. I know you all have felt this battle before.

- What does it feel like when that battle is going on in your life? *(Not good. I feel like I can't win and do what's right. I get irritated.)*

- What are some of the things you struggle with that you know you shouldn't do? *(I lie to my mom sometimes. I get angry and hit my little brother. When I get mad, I swear sometimes.)*

Think about some changes you would like to see in you life now that you are a Christian. Write down two changes you would like to make, one on each wing of your butterfly. **Hand out the card stock paper.** Glue your butterfly body on this card, leaving the wings free. Use your felt-tip marker to add eyes and antennae.

When everyone has finished, have the students talk to God and ask Him to help them make these changes in their life.

MEMORY VERSE ACTIVITY: Old Nature/New Nature

2 Corinthians 5:17—"Therefore, if anyone is in Christ, / he is a new creation; / the old has gone, / the new has come!"

Write the verse on the board in parts as shown. Say together once. Divide your class into four groups and have members of each group sit together. Assign each group one of the above phrases. When you point to each group, have them say their phrase.

Repeat by giving groups different phrases. When your students know the verse well, try the response another way. Erase the verse from the board. Assign each group a number from 1 to 4. Have students sit in random order so they are not sitting in groups. Call out the number of each group in order and see if the students can remember to respond with their group.

WEEKLY ASSIGNMENT: Butterfly Beginning

Make sure each student has his or her butterfly card. Take your butterfly home and put it on your bulletin board or another place where you will see it every day. Each day, ask God to help you make the changes you wrote on your butterfly.

New Creatures

Houseflies—The taste-sensitive cells of the common housefly are located on its feet as well as on its mouthparts. The female housefly lays an average of 150 white eggs in a mass about 1 mm long. The eggs are laid in manure or other decaying substances. The female lives about 2½ months and lays between 600 and 1,000 eggs during her lifetime. The eggs hatch in about 12 hours into white, legless larvae called maggots, which grow to 12.5 mm in length. The maggot goes through the pupa stage in five to six days. The new adult emerges in another four to five days if the weather is warm or in a month or later if weather conditions are unfavorable. On average, 12 generations of houseflies are produced in one year.

Mosquitoes—They are found from the tropics to the Arctic Circle and from lowlands to the peaks of high mountains. They have long, slender wings and have small scales over most of the wing veins. The body is narrow. The long antennae have numerous whorls of hair. In some types of mosquitoes, the mouthparts of the female are long, adapted for piercing and for sucking blood. The male, which feeds on nectar and water, has rudimentary mouthparts. Females of this group prefer the blood of warm-blooded animals. When mosquitoes bite, they inject some of their saliva into the wound, causing swelling and irritation. Many inject infectious microorganisms and thus transmit diseases.

Female mosquitoes lay their eggs only in water; some species lay their eggs in running water, others in woodland pools, marshes, swamps, estuaries, or in containers such as rain barrels. The larvae are known as wrigglers because of their wriggling motion in the water. A large number of mosquito eggs and larvae are destroyed by small fish.

Monarch Butterfly—The monarch occurs throughout the world, mainly in North America. The adult has wings of a striking reddish-brown, with black veins and black borders with two rows of white dots. The wingspread is 4 inches. Each fall the monarch butterfly migrates south to California, Florida, and Mexico. The longest flight known for a tagged adult is some 1,800 miles from Ontario to Mexico. Migratory groups congregate at the same places each winter, such as Pacific Grove, California, or the mountains in central Mexico, where the trees may be completely covered with monarchs. In its average two-year lifetime, the individual makes the trip twice. The females lay their eggs on the underside of milkweed leaves. The larvae feed on the milkweed plants and accumulate a poisonous substance that makes them distasteful to birds and other predators. The birds learn to recognize the butterflies' bright wing pattern and avoid them.

Digging Up the Dirt

LESSON PLAN

OBJECTIVE: Students will evaluate their relationship with God through learning about the parable of the soil and seeds.

APPLICATION: Students will decide on three ways to produce fruit in their lives and how to implement them at home.

LESSON PLAN ELEMENT	ACTIVITY	TIME	SUPPLIES
Opening Activity	*Sizing Up Seeds*	7–10	4 empty egg cartons; 4 copies of "Sizing Up Seeds" handout; large bag of M&Ms; 4 rolls of masking tape; 4 paper cups; 4 blue, 4 yellow, 4 orange, and 4 brown markers
Bible Story—Matthew 13:1–23, parable of the good soil	*All Soiled Up*	10–15	Bible; 4 types of soil (see activity)
Check for Understanding	*Sizing Up the Soil*	3–5	"Sizing Up Seeds" handouts; pencils
Memory Verse Activity	*Sowing Seeds*	3–5	3 to 4 small containers (1 for each team); 10"×2" strips of paper (8 for each team); felt-tip markers or pens; cellophane tape
Lesson Activity	*Garden Tools*	7–10	Bibles; 3 slips of paper; 4 copies of "Garden Tools" handout; pencils
Application	*Producing Fruit*	7–10	Bibles; "Garden Tools" handouts; pencils
Weekly Assignment	*Good Gardening*	3–5	"Garden Tools" handouts

At the time Jesus told His parables, His listeners lived close to nature. Many either farmed the land or were related to farmers. Dry conditions meant less food for the entire village. More rain and good growing conditions meant bountiful living.

Today, youngsters are less likely to connect abundant resources with God's provision of rain, sunshine, and good soil. However, many probably have tried to grow plants in school, have studied the biology of plant life, and may even have helped their parents plant flowers, water the grass, or watch vegetables ripen.

For this lesson, you will need to tailor your comments to the group you teach. If you live in farm country, bring the resources around you to help your students learn the principle Jesus was teaching. If you live in the city, find creative ways to link the parable of the good soil to your students' lives.

This lesson asks your students to appraise their heart attitudes. Emphasize that this appraisal is very personal and that only God and you know the condition of your heart. Do not allow students to comment on the kind of "soil" in another person's heart.

The parable of the good soil is so simple that your students will grasp it quickly. But they will interact with the principles even more deeply if you bring soil for them to touch, smell, and see.

LESSON PLAN

OPENING ACTIVITY: Sizing Up Seeds

Before Class: Examine the egg cartons to ensure there are no holes large enough to allow M&Ms to fall through. The students will be shaking M&Ms inside the cartons, so tape or glue paper over all open spaces. Using a marker, number the bottom of each egg cup from 1 to 12. It's best to scatter the numbers instead of numbering consecutively. Place 12 blue, 12 yellow, 12 brown, and 12 orange M&Ms in each paper cup.

To begin your class, discuss what changes your students are making concerning the ideas they wrote on their butterflies. Encourage students to be specific on what they did to make those changes and how God helped them do it.

When you are ready to begin the Opening Activity, divide students into groups of four. Give each group a cup of M&Ms, an egg carton, and a roll of masking tape.

- What are some things that make a seed grow? *(Sunlight; water; good soil; air.)*

If a seed has all these things it will become a healthy plant.

We are going to do an activity to see the probability of a seed growing in different places. We will record our results on this chart. **Give each group a "Sizing Up Seeds" handout and a yellow, blue, orange, and brown marker.**

We are going to think about what might happen to seeds that are planted in different kinds of soil. Let's pretend that we have planted seeds in our egg cartons. Will they grow? What do they need to grow well?

Numbers 1, 2, and 3 in your carton will represent seeds planted by the roadside or on a well-traveled path. This path has hard dirt in it. Look for these numbers in your egg carton.

Numbers 4, 5, and 6 represent seeds that are planted in rocky soil. Find these numbers in your carton.

Numbers 7, 8, and 9 will represent soil that is covered by tall thorns or weeds. Locate these numbers in your egg carton.

Finally, numbers 10, 11, and 12 will represent those seeds planted in rich garden soil.

Now we must add the necessary elements that seeds need to grow. We will let the M&Ms represent the things that seeds need to produce healthy plants.

Take your 12 orange M&Ms. They represent good, clean air. All the seeds are in places where good air is accessible. Spread the 12 orange M&Ms on the inside cover of your egg carton. Now close the cover and shake the carton well. When finished, open the carton. Look at where the M&Ms landed and record it on your chart by coloring in one square for each M&M. **Give students time to do this.**

Now set your orange M&Ms aside. Take your 12 yellow M&Ms. These represent sunshine.

- Is there a group of seeds that might not get much sunshine? *(The thorny soil seeds.)*

The thorns block out much of the sun. Find numbers 7, 8, and 9. Take your masking tape and tape an X over the opening of each of these numbers. These seeds will get some sunshine but their probability is lessened. **Give groups time to do this.**

Now put your 12 yellow M&Ms on the inside cover. Close the cover and shake. Open the cover and record your findings on your chart, using your yellow marker this time. **Give groups time to do this.**

Now set your yellow M&Ms aside and take your 12 blue ones. These represent water.

- Is there a group of seeds that might not get as much water? *(The hard path.)*

The water will run off the hard dirt and have a tough time soaking in. Find numbers 1, 2, and 3. Take the tape off numbers 7, 8, and 9, and tape an X over numbers 1, 2, and 3. **Give groups time to do this.**

Now put your 12 blue M&Ms on the inside cover. Close the cover and shake. Open the cover and record your findings using a blue marker. **Give groups time to do this.**

Now set your blue M&Ms aside and take out the 12 brown ones. These represent the minerals found in rich soil.

- Is there a group of seeds that might not get as many minerals? *(The rocky soil.)*

The rocky soil has fewer minerals because of all the rocks it contains. Find numbers 4, 5, and 6. Take the masking tape off 1, 2, and 3, and tape an X over 4, 5, and 6. Now place your brown M&Ms on the cover, close it, and shake. Open the cover and use your brown marker to record the results on your chart. **Give groups time to do this.**

Let's compare our results. As we discussed earlier, a seed needs all four things—sun, water, air, and minerals to grow. Look at your chart. Which numbers received all four? **As each group reports their results, tally the numbers on the board. The majority of the numbers should be 10, 11, and 12.**

The seed that has been planted in the good garden soil has the best chance to grow. Did you know that Jesus compared our hearts to these four kinds of soil? Let's listen to our Bible lesson to discover what He said about it.

Allow students to eat their M&Ms.

BIBLE STORY: All Soiled Up

Before Class: Bring samples of the four different types of soil. In a large zip-lock baggie, put dry soil with lots of rocks. In a second bag, put good, moist garden loam. Firmly pack clay soil into a pie plate or a bread loaf pan. In a third zip-lock bag, place soil with lots of thorny weeds. (If you are unable to get weeds, cut out a picture and enclose it in the bag.)

Have students sit in a circle. Have you ever planted a garden and then worked in it to grow plants? Lots of people love to see healthy flowers, vegetables, trees, and other plants growing in their yards or gardens. They spend much time preparing the soil before they plant their seeds.

- What kinds of tools do you use in a garden? *(Hoes, shovels, rakes, rototillers.)*

- What do these tools do? *(Hoes dig out weeds. Shovels turn over the soil to make it looser. Rakes smooth out the soil. Rototillers grind up the soil to make it easier to plant.)*

As we learned in our Opening Activity, seeds need good conditions for growing. They need plenty of good air, sunshine, clean water, and minerals. If you have ever planted a garden in soil that didn't allow the plants to get enough of these elements, your plants probably didn't do well. They may even have died.

Jesus told many parables. These are stories with a lesson in them. Let's read the parable Jesus told about the soil. **Read Matthew 13:1–9. As you come to each type of soil, hold up the sample and pass it around the circle. Let students open the bags and touch the soil.**

Then Jesus explained what the parable meant. **Read Matthew 13:18–23. You may wish to pass around each type of soil again as it is mentioned.**

Let me see if you remember the facts of the story. **Ask the following questions, bringing out the main idea in your discussion.**

- Who is the sower or planter? *(God.)*

- What is the seed? *(The Word of God.)*

- Who do the birds represent? *(The evil one or the devil.)*

- What does the soil represent? *(Our hearts.)*

- What does the hard path represent? *(A hard heart that doesn't understand God's Word.)*

- What does the rocky soil represent? *(The person who is excited about God's Word at first but only for a short time. When hard times come, he turns away from God's Word.)*

- What does the thorny soil represent? *(The person who lets the things in this world like riches or worries take the place of God's Word.)*

- Who does the good soil represent? *(The person who takes in God's Word and grows spiritually. He produces lots of good works in his life.)*

In this lesson, we'll be looking at our hearts to see what kind of soil we represent. Are you like the hard path with a hard heart? Or like the rocky soil with no roots in God's Word? Or the thorny soil that lets other things take the place of God's Word? Or the good soil that allows God's Word to help you grow?

CHECK FOR UNDERSTANDING: Sizing Up the Soil

Make sure each student has a pencil and their own "Sizing Up Seeds" handout. Have students write in the correct answers below each type of heart under the section "Sizing Up Soil."

Sowing good seeds results in a good harvest. Sowing bad seeds results in a bad harvest. Let's learn a verse that gives us this principle.

MEMORY VERSE ACTIVITY: Sowing Seeds

Galatians 6:7—"Do not be deceived; / God cannot be mocked. / A man reaps / what he sows."

Write the verse on the board, dividing it into phrases as shown. Divide students into three or four groups. Give each group four strips of paper, a small container, and a felt-tip marker or pen. Set out the tape.

This verse refers to soil and planting seeds. If you plant carrot seeds, you will get carrots, not watermelons. The same is true for our spiritual life. If we plant evil by saying mean things to others, we will reap evil when people do the same back to us. If we smile, people will return our smiles.

Let's read this verse together. **Do this several times.** In your group, write each of the four phrases of this verse on a separate strip of paper, dividing the verse as shown on the board. Roll up each strip so the writing cannot be seen, and tape the end. Place all four rolls into your container. **Give groups time to do this.**

We have now planted our seeds in the containers. We will reap them in a few minutes. The goal for each team is to get a whole verse assembled before the other teams.

First, select a team member to take a turn. I will read one of the phrases, leaving out a word. The four chosen team members must say the word before the other team members. The person who says the word the quickest must then repeat the phrase correctly. If the phrase is correct, the team member will choose a roll of paper from the group's container and tape it to the board. Each team should tape their strips to a different section of the board so that the strips don't get mixed up. The first team with an assembled verse wins.

Select a representative from each team to compete. Begin with the first phrase. You might say, "Do be deceived." The first person to say "not" wins. He or she repeats, "Do not be deceived." If the phrase is repeated correctly, the team member selects a strip of paper and tapes it to the board. Then have newly selected representatives compete with another phrase. Team members need to tape their strips on the board in the right order. When one team has put all four strips in order, recite the verse together again. Ask for volunteers to say the verse.

Now let's look at some tools to help us reap a good harvest.

LESSON ACTIVITY: Garden Tools

 Before Class: Write these verses on slips of paper:
The Roadside Path (see Matthew 13:4,18,19), Hebrews 3:15 and Romans 10:17;
The Rocky Ground (see Matthew 13:5,6,20,21), 1 Corinthians 10:13 and Proverbs 29:25;
The Thorny Soil (see Matthew 13:7,22), 1 Peter 5:7 and Matthew 6:19–21.

Divide students into three groups: the Roadside Crew, the Rock Pickers, and the Weed Pullers. Give each group a copy of the "Garden Tools" handout and the slip of paper that goes along with the group's title. Make sure students have Bibles and a pencil.

In your group, you will be answering this question: How can this type of soil be changed so it is good for growing? The answers will come from your Bible verses.

Read the verses. Then decide as a group what the verses say about making bad soil into good soil. On your "Garden Tools" handout, write how you would use each tool. For example, the Thorny Soil group could write "dig out the weeds of worries in your life" beside the shovel. I will give you five minutes to read, think, and write.

While students are working, circulate to help them come up with good ideas. The following are some suggestions:

The Roadside Crew:

> *Hoe—soften up the soil of our hard hearts*
> *Hose—water our lives with the Word of God*
> *Shovel—dig up all the hard, rebellious thoughts*

The Rock Pickers:

> *Hoe—hoe up all the sin-rocks*
> *Hose—wash away all the fear so we can trust God*
> *Shovel—shovel away all the sin*

The Weed Pullers:

> *Hoe—chop up all my worries*
> *Hose—wash away love for things and love God instead*
> *Shovel—pile up treasures in heaven rather than on earth*

Have groups report on what their verses said and explain how they would use each garden tool.

It takes a lot of work to prepare soil. Any gardener knows that. But the results are worth it. Once we have good soil, we can then plant the seeds of God's Word and watch them grow. Our hearts will be prepared to let God's Word work in our lives.

APPLICATION: Producing Fruit

Give each student a personal copy of the "Garden Tools" handout and make sure each person has a Bible and a pencil.

Now let's see what we can do to plant God's Word in our lives. **Have a good reader read Mark 4:20 and Luke 8:15.**

- How does Mark 4:20 describe our Christian growth when we have good soil in our hearts? *(We will produce lots of fruit. We will grow very fast and very good.)*

- What kind of person is described in Luke 8:15? *(A person who has a good heart. Someone who hears God's Word and remembers what it says.)*

Have a good reader read 2 Peter 1:5–7.

- What kind of spiritual fruit or good works are named in these verses? *(Faith; goodness; knowledge; self-control; perseverance; godliness; brotherly kindness; love.)*

Write the kinds of fruit on the board as they are mentioned. When these things grow in your heart, you become more and more like Jesus. People notice the change in your life and you are able to share about God's love with others.

Jesus tells us in John 15:16: **Read the verse.** This fruit can refer either to good works or to introducing others to Jesus as their Savior. Bearing fruit is our main job as believers.

Look at your "Garden Tools" handout. For the next few moments, I want you to write down three things that you need to do to grow spiritually. Write one thing next to each tool. For example, you might write, "I need to wash away the bad language I use," or, "I need to dig out my bad attitude about not wanting to go to church." Then beside each tool, draw a piece of fruit, such as an apple, pear, or grapes. Write the spiritual fruit that you want to produce by using your tool. For example, "Washing away bad language" could result in self-control. You would write self-control beside the fruit you drew. And changing a bad attitude about church could result in more love for God. These are things you will work on this week.

Give students time to reflect and write. God's Word is our best tool. Using the verses we read in our lesson, write one that applies to each problem you listed on your worksheet. I will list them on the board so you can look them up if you need to remind yourself of what they say.

Write on the board: Matthew 13:4–7,18–22; Hebrews 3:15; Romans 10:17; 1 Corinthians 10:13; Proverbs 29:25; 1 Peter 5:7; Matthew 6:19–21; Mark 4:20; Luke 8:15; 2 Peter 1:5–7; John 15:16. Help students who are having difficulties relating the Bible references to the problems they wrote on their handout.

WEEKLY ASSIGNMENT: Good Gardening

Take your "Garden Tools" handouts home with you. This week, work on the areas you wrote next to your tools. As you do, you will be making your heart soften toward God and His Word. When we meet for our next session, plan to share the results of your "good gardening" with the class.

Sizing Up Seeds

Hard Path			Rocky Soil			Thorny Soil			Good Soil		
Seed 1	Seed 2	Seed 3	Seed 4	Seed 5	Seed 6	Seed 7	Seed 8	Seed 9	Seed 10	Seed 11	Seed 12

Sizing Up Soil

Can you remember the kinds of soil? Below each heart, write the type of soil that is represented.

_____   _____   _____   _____

Garden Tools

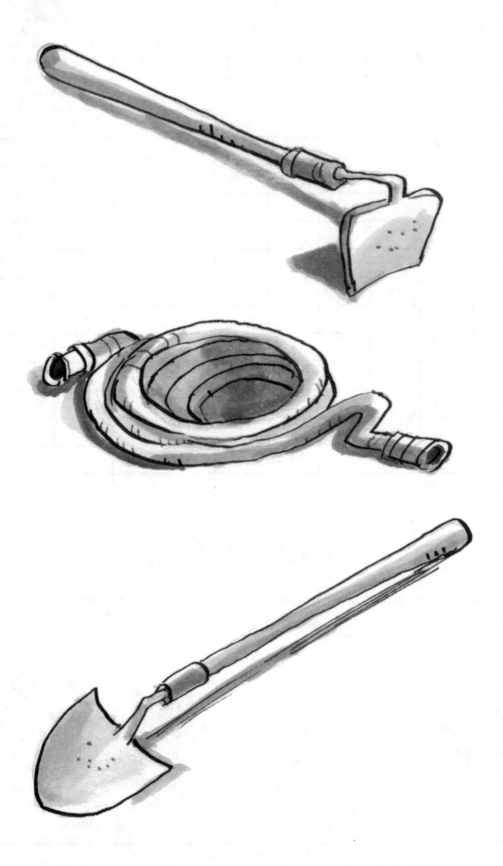

Wipe It Clean!

LESSON PLAN

OBJECTIVE: Students will learn the importance of living the cleansed life moment by moment.

APPLICATION: Students will make a record of the wrongs they have committed, confess these sins to God, and destroy the list to signify God's forgiveness.

LESSON PLAN ELEMENT	ACTIVITY	TIME	SUPPLIES
Opening Activity	*Wiped Clean*	7–10	Clear contact paper; "Record of Wrongs" handouts; overhead or dry-erase markers (1 for each student); water; paper towels; tissues; spray cleaner; cleaning rag
Bible Story—2 Samuel 11:22–12:13, David and Bathsheba	*Secret Sins*	10–15	Bible; "Record of Wrongs" clipboards; dark-colored markers; tissues
Check for Understanding	*Getting to the Left Circle*	3–5	
Lesson Activity	*Attitude Makes the Difference*	7–10	Bible; situation cards from the "Attitude Makes the Difference" handout; pencils; glue or tape; 18 index cards
Application	*Cleansing Power*	7–10	Bible; "Record of Wrongs" clipboards; dark-colored markers; tissues
Memory Verse Activity	*Right Writings*	3–5	Markers; "Right from Wrong" clipboards; 4 large paper strips or posters
Weekly Assignment	*A Clean Slate*	3–5	"Record of Wrongs" clipboard; dark-colored markers; optional: stapler, ribbon, craft magnets

Have you ever asked yourself, "If the Holy Spirit was sent to give me power to live a victorious life, why do I feel so powerless, so defeated?" We often yearn for spiritual power and do not have it because of impure motives, selfish desires, or unconfessed sin. God does not fill a dirty vessel with His power and love. The vessel of our lives must be cleansed by the blood of our Lord before it can be filled with the Spirit of God.

The psalmist wrote, "Search me, O God, and know my heart; test me and know my anxious thoughts. See if there is any offensive way in me, and lead me in the way everlasting" (Psalm 139:23,24).

This prayer is an essential discipline of the Christian's inner life. It expresses to God our desire for purity, our longing to make His ways our ways. Asking Him to reveal to us any unconfessed sin enables us to keep our accounts short with Him. Confession results in cleansing. God's Word promises, "If we confess our sins, he is faithful and just and will forgive us our sins and purify us from all unrighteousness" (1 John 1:9).

The Holy Spirit longs to fill us with His power and love. In this lesson, your students will learn how their lives can have this power. The first step is to be cleansed from sin and filled with the Spirit of God.

LESSON PLAN

OPENING ACTIVITY: Wiped Clean

Before Class: Cut the contact paper into 8½"×11" pieces, allowing two pieces for each student. Set out small bowls of water for students to dip paper towels into while cleaning. Locate spots of dirt around your room that you will be able to clean quickly. You may want to create "dirty" areas to make the demonstration more dramatic.

Share the results of the "good gardening" your students did for the previous lesson's weekly assignment.

When all the students have gathered, give each student a paper towel and have them look for spots that need cleaning. Go around the room, cleaning the dirty areas you have noticed or planted. Make a big production out of it by saying things like "Oh, my! How did this get here?" "Well, now, I've never seen such a mess!" "Oh, I'm glad I got this spot before it got too large."

When finished cleaning, have students look at their paper towels and your cloth. **Comment,** Wow! Can you believe all the dirt we found in here today? Look at this cloth. It shows what a mess our room was in. Sometimes we don't even realize how dirty our room has become.

This is true of our lives too. We learned that after we invited Christ to come into our lives, we became a new creature in Christ. But we also will still do wrong things. Sin messes up our hearts and cuts off our communication with God. But God allows us to wipe away these sins from our clean life. Let's do an activity to help us understand this.

Distribute the "Record of Wrongs" handout, scissors, clear contact paper, and tissues. **Have students make boards by covering them with contact paper—back and front—and cutting them out to look like a clipboard. Give each student a dry-erase marker. They will take these home at the end of the class.**

Teaching Tip: To apply the contact paper, have students carefully remove the protective paper from one piece and lay the contact paper on the table with the sticky side up. Lay the paper board on it, then take the protective paper off the other sheet and lay it on top of the board. Trim the edges. If markers are not available for students to keep, use crayons.

When students are finished, read 1 John 1:9. When we have sin in our life, God can erase it for us when we confess it to Him. Take your marker and write one sin on your board that someone your age might do. It could be getting angry and hitting someone, telling a lie, or taking something that belongs to someone else. **Give students time to do this.** Now take a tissue and wipe it away. **Give students time to do this.** This is a good illustration of how God deals with confessed sin. Let's listen to a Bible story to help us understand more about confessed sin.

BIBLE STORY: Secret Sins

The Bible story is about David and Bathsheba. Due to the sensitive nature of the topic presented, omit the details of David's adultery. Some of your students will not be able to handle this kind of information. But all your students can understand the sin of wanting another person's spouse.

Have you ever done something wrong, really wrong, that you thought no one knew about? Have you ever tried to hide what you did from everyone, including your parents and friends?

- How does it feel to do something wrong and not tell anyone? *(It feels like something is heavy inside me. I don't like that feeling.)*

- What sometimes happens when you hide a sin? *(You get caught later. You do more sin to cover it up.)*

Sometimes even people who love God get caught up in sin. Once you commit one sin and don't confess it to God, you may commit another sin to cover up the first sin. Soon, your sin is so deep that you can't get out of it. It's like getting stuck in a mud hole—the more you struggle to get out, the deeper into the mud you get.

In our Bible story, we're going to hear about someone who was faithful to God, but then let sin get into his life—with terrible consequences. He let sin rule his life.

Make sure your students have their "Record of Wrongs" clipboards, tissues, and markers. King David is the man we're going to hear about today. He loved God and God considered him a friend. But David did something very terrible. As I tell the story, I want you to write down, on your "Record of Wrongs" board, each sin that David committed and didn't tell anyone about. When we finish the story, we'll look at your lists.

Tell the following story in your own words. David had a lot of power. He was the king of the land and his people loved him. He was brave in battle, always led his troops onto the battlefield, took good care of his kingdom, and served God. He seemed to have it all.

But then he started cutting corners. His army was engaged in battle with the fierce Ammonites who wanted to destroy the Israelite nation. David and his army destroyed the Ammonite army. Then David sent his army out to surround the city of Rabbah. He put Joab, his best commander, in charge of the army. But David didn't go with his troops. He decided to stay in Jerusalem in the palace and take it easy. After all, the hard part of the battle was done. He didn't need to be with his troops anymore. Joab could do the job.

While David was in Jerusalem, he noticed a very beautiful woman. He wondered who she was, so he asked someone. The man said, "Her name is Bathsheba. She's the wife of Uriah the Hittite, a man who serves in your army."

David knew that he shouldn't be looking at someone else's wife. But he wanted Bathsheba as his own wife. He couldn't stop thinking about her. He talked to Bathsheba and found out that she liked him too.

Then David devised a plan. If Bathsheba weren't married, David could marry her.

David called for his general, Joab. He said, "Joab, put Uriah on the front lines where the fighting is the fiercest. Then when he starts fighting the enemy, pull back the rest of the troops so that Uriah is there all by himself. Then he will be killed by the enemy."

Joab obeyed King David. He placed Uriah where the fighting was the heaviest. Before the battle was over, Uriah was dead. He died for a very bad reason—David's desire to have what didn't belong to him.

Joab sent a messenger to David to report on the battle. He told the messenger, "Tell King David about the battle. Explain that I sent some men very close to the city wall. Some died from arrows that were shot from the city wall. Others died from heavy things being thrown down on top of them. The king may get mad because so many soldiers were killed. He may ask you, 'Why did Joab send these men so close to the wall?' If he does, tell him, 'Uriah the Hittite is dead too.' Then King David will not be mad."

That's just what the messenger did. This is what happened. **Read 2 Samuel 11:22–25.**

When Bathsheba heard about her husband's death, she cried and was very sad. After a while, David brought her to the palace and married her. David seemed to have gotten away with his sin. No one knew what he had done except Joab and Bathsheba. David still looked like the good king.

But God knew. God knows all our sin. He is not surprised at what we do. He knows all about the bad attitudes and secret sins that lurk in our hearts.

God wasn't going to let David get away with his sin. God sent a prophet named Nathan to talk to David. Nathan told David a story. **Read 2 Samuel 12:1–4.**

Look at David's reaction to the story. **Read 2 Samuel 12:5,6.**

What David didn't know was that the story represented his own life. David got upset over the sin of other people, but he didn't get upset over his own sin.

Then Nathan told David what God thought of his sin. **Read 2 Samuel 12:7–9.** Who had blessed David? God had. Who had made David a powerful king? God had. David had every-thing he wanted—except Uriah's wife. So David took that too.

This was David's reaction: **Read 2 Samuel 12:13.** David was truly sorry for his sin. He repented; he confessed his sins.

- What sins did you write on your clipboard? What sins did David commit that he hid from his people? (*Use this progression of sins to fill in the discussion: unfaithfulness when he didn't go to war with his troops; covetousness when he wanted Uriah's wife; murder when he had Uriah killed in battle; hardness of heart when he didn't admit his sin right away; unjust anger when he wanted the man in the story to be punished but didn't regard his own sin.)*

When we don't confess our sins to God right away, we end up sinning more and more. One sin leads to another. Our lives sink deeper and deeper into the mud hole of sin.

- What might have happened if David had confessed his sin of unfaithfulness when he stayed in Jerusalem instead of leading his troops? *(He would have gone back to the battle site and not seen Bathsheba.)*

- What might have happened if David had confessed his sin when he first wanted Bathsheba as his wife? *(He wouldn't have had Uriah killed.)*

- What might have happened if David had confessed his sin after he told Joab to put Uriah in the front lines of battle? *(He might have been able to cancel the order in time to save Uriah's life.)*

- How do you think David felt when Nathan told him that the person in the story who had stolen the sheep was really David himself? *(He saw all the bad things he had done and realized how bad they really were. He suddenly knew that God had seen him do all those terrible things.)*

Once David confessed his sin to God and was sorry about what he had done, God forgave his sin. That is called God's cleansing. God cleaned the guilt out of David's heart. Although David still had to suffer the consequences of his sin, he could once again walk and talk with God. To show what God did with David's sins when David confessed them to God, erase the list of David's sins.

In our Lesson Activity, we will investigate our own sins and what we must do to keep ourselves from getting too far into sin. But first, let's use what we know about the Life Circles to describe what happened to David.

CHECK FOR UNDERSTANDING: Getting to the Left Circle
Draw the following diagram on the chalkboard as you explain the concept.

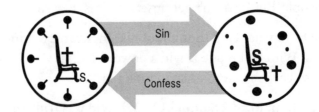

David's experience shows us what happens when believers sin. When we don't have sin in our lives, we are like the Spiritual Christian circle. **Have a volunteer come to the board and draw the left circle on the board. Have students call out the details to put into the circle (the cross, "s," and orderly dots).** When we have sin in our lives, we're like the Worldly Christian. **Have another volunteer come to the board and draw the right circle on the board. Have students call out the details to put into the circle (the cross, "s," and disorder-**

ly dots). **If you have time, have students tell you which characteristics go with each circle.**

When we sin, we go from this circle to that one. **Draw the "sin" arrow.** There is only one way to get back from the wrong circle to the correct circle—through confession. Confession is agreeing with God about our sins and asking Him to forgive them. **Draw the "confess" arrow.**

LESSON ACTIVITY: Attitude Makes the Difference

 Before Class: Make one photocopy of "Attitude Makes the Difference." Cut apart the situation cards.

When it comes to sin, attitude makes the difference. When your attitude is right, you'll do what's right. When your attitude is wrong, you'll do what's wrong.

- What are some attitudes that would go against God's standards? (*Bring out these attitudes, along with others: selfishness; greediness; gloominess; anger; pride; unloving.*)

- What attitudes did you see in David when he sinned? (*Unloving; laziness; selfishness; greediness.*)

God promises that He will help us with any temptation we have. **Read 1 Corinthians 10:13.** Bad attitudes that we don't get rid of are sin. Usually, this is how sin happens. First, you are tempted. You have a bad attitude in the area of the temptation. You sin. Then you must deal with your sin.

Let me give you an example. Jennifer loves Barbie dolls. She plays with them all the time. When she visits Tasha, she plays with Tasha's Barbies. Tasha has a gown for her Barbie that Jennifer loves. It is a soft green with gems all over the skirt. One day when she is at Tasha's house, Tasha tells her that she lost the green gown. Then Tasha goes to the kitchen to fix Jennifer a snack. While she is gone, Jennifer notices the green gown hidden underneath Tasha's dresser—a place where Tasha will probably not find it for a long time.

Jennifer thinks, *I could take it home and Tasha would never know.* Jennifer has just been tempted to do something wrong. She also thinks, *Tasha has so many Barbie clothes that she'll never miss one. And her mom will buy her another one any time she asks, so it's okay to take it.* Jennifer's attitude is wrong because she doesn't respect Tasha's belongings. She is envious of something Tasha has, and is greedy because she wants it for her own.

So Jennifer puts the gown in her Barbie bag and takes it home. Tasha never knows. That's the sin.

- What could Jennifer do after she gets home to make things right with God and with Tasha? (*She should admit to God that what she did was wrong and ask for forgiveness, and then take the dress back to Tasha and ask for her forgiveness.*)

- What should Jennifer's attitude have been to start with? (*That Tasha's things belong to her no matter how many Barbie clothes Tasha has. That stealing is always wrong.*)

- What could have happened if Jennifer had the right attitude? *(She would have shown Tasha that she found her Barbie gown, so her friend would be happy. She would not take the dress home.)*

Let me explain something about what happens when Christians sin. Jesus paid for all your sins when He died on the cross. That includes the sins you committed in the past, the ones you are doing right now, and the ones you will do in the future. Because you accepted Jesus' payment for your sins, you will never have to pay for those sins with eternal punishment in hell.

But when you sin, your relationship with God changes. It's like what happens in your family. You will always be a part of your family no matter what you do. But when you do something wrong, your communication with your parents changes. You can't run up to them and talk to them like you did before. You must first tell them you were wrong and ask for their forgiveness. Then things will be right again.

That's how it is with God. He always loves us—even when we sin. But our fellowship with Him is damaged when we sin. We must confess our sin to Him and He will cleanse our sin. Then our relationship with Him becomes good again.

Now we will do presentations that show good and bad attitudes. **Divide students into six groups. Give each group one of the situation cards from the "Attitude Makes the Difference" handout, a pencil, glue or tape, and three index cards.**

In your group, glue (tape) your situation onto an index card. Then read your situation. Decide which bad attitude is shown by the main character. Write that attitude on the second index card. On the back of that card, write what might happen because of that bad attitude.

On the third card, write the attitude that would result if the main character confessed his or her bad attitude and asked God to give him or her a good attitude. Then, on the back of that card, write what might happen because of the new attitude. When you finish, you will present your ideas to the class.

Give students time to write. Circulate to help them think through their situations and the good and bad attitudes. Suggested answers are:

1. Bad attitude: *disobedience*

   What might happen: *Jason's parents will be disappointed because he wants to go against their wishes.*

   Good attitude: *obedience*

   What might happen: *Jason will go to boys' club and learn more about Jesus, and have fun too!*

2. Bad attitude: *jealousy*

   What might happen: *Jasmine creates fights in her family.*

   Good attitude: *unselfishness*

What might happen: *Because Jasmine acts so kindly to her brother and sister, her older brother lets her go with him to a baseball game and her younger sister gives her a big hug. Jasmine feels happy.*

3. Bad attitude: *rebelliousness*

    What might happen: *Robbie and his stepmother get into a fight.*

    Good attitude: *obeying those in authority*

    What might happen: *Robbie and his stepmother learn to get along better, causing more harmony in the family.*

4. Bad attitude: *unthankfulness*

    What might happen: *Chris never enjoys his bike and his parents are disappointed in him for his bad attitude.*

    Good attitude: *thankfulness*

    What might happen: *Chris enjoys his bike and his parents are so pleased with his attitude that they get him a new helmet to go with his new bike.*

5. Bad attitude: *snobbiness*

    What might happen: *All the kids in Julie's class consider her a snob.*

    Good attitude: *helpfulness*

    What might happen: *Julie helps Lisa and others and gets a reputation as a person who cares about other people, not just herself.*

6. Bad attitude: *lack of compassion*

    What might happen: *Matthew's attitude rubs off on others at school and lots of people avoid Melissa.*

    Good attitude: *loving*

    What might happen: *Because of Matthew's attention to Melissa, other people help her too and include her in their groups.*

When students finish, have one person in each group read the group's situation, another person explain the bad attitude and what might happen, and a third person give the good attitude and what might happen. (If there are fewer than three students in a group, double up on responsibilities.)

Teaching Tip: If you have time, play a game with the index cards. Mix up the situations cards and place them in a pile. Mix up the good and bad attitude cards and place them in another pile. Have students draw a situation card and match it up with the bad attitude and good attitude related to that situation.

Remember, the pattern for committing sin is being tempted, have an attitude problem, and then sinning. Having a good attitude makes the difference. It breaks the pattern of sin. However, many times we will not have the right attitude and will fall into sin. Just as David did, we may find ourselves tangled up in bad consequences and hurt ourselves and others. Jesus wants to cleanse us of our sins. In our Application, we'll find out how we can be cleansed from our sins.

APPLICATION: Cleansing Power

Make sure your students have their "Record of Wrongs" clipboards, dark-colored markers, and clean tissues.

Now we come to the part that you can do. God is waiting to cleanse your sins. His desire is for you to walk and talk with Him every day. He doesn't want anything to come between you and Him. The Book of Proverbs tells us what happens if we don't confess our sins. **Read Proverbs 28:13.**

- In what ways will you not prosper if you don't confess your sin? *(You will suffer bad consequences. You will not be able to talk to God like you want to. You will get further into sin.)*

- If you tell lies, how will you suffer bad consequences? *(Your lies will get you into trouble. You will develop a habit of always lying.)*

- If you steal things, how will you suffer bad consequences? *(You will get a reputation as a thief. You might end up in jail. People won't trust you.)*

- If you talk disrespectfully to your parents, how will you suffer bad consequences? *(Your parents might ground you. Your parents won't buy you nice things.)*

At times, we all let our wrongdoing come between us and God. We must develop a habit of confessing our sin as soon as it happens.

Let's imagine that you have a new white T-shirt that you love. It rained earlier in the day. You go outside and your dog jumps up on you. His muddy paws leave smears on the front of your brand new shirt.

If you have helped your mother wash the laundry, you may know that the longer you leave stains on clothing, the harder they are to get out. When your mother sees your stained shirt, she will probably wash it immediately. She wants to take care of the stain right away.

That's what you should do with your sin. Immediately ask God to cleanse it. You should want to get rid of your sin right away.

There are three steps to being cleansed by God:

1. Confess your sin. Confessing your sin means agreeing with God that it is wrong. Tell God exactly what you did wrong.

2. Agree with God that Jesus paid for that sin on the cross.

3. Repent—change your attitude toward that sin, which means you will change your actions too.

David learned a lot about confession. Let's read what he tells us to do. **Read Psalm 32. After each set of verses listed, discuss the question.**

- (Verses 1,2) Who does God bless? *(Those people who have their sins forgiven.)*

- (Verses 3,4) How did David describe the time when he kept sinning and didn't confess his sins? *(He felt like his bones were wasting away. He hurt a lot from the guilt. He groaned all day long. He didn't have much strength.)*

David gave a good description of what happens when we keep sinning yet don't confess it to God. We become miserable.

- (Verse 5) What action did David take? *(He confessed his sin to God.)*

- (Verses 6,7) What will God do for those who confess their sins? *(Protect them.)*

- (Verses 8–12) How does David describe people who keep on sinning? *(Like a horse or mule that needs to have something in its mouth to control them. They don't have any understanding. They have lots of troubles.)*

- (Verses 8–12) How does David describe the person who trusts in God? *(God will teach them and watch over them. God's love surrounds them. They will rejoice and be glad.)*

I am going to give each of you a few moments to pray and confess your sins to God. Take your "Record of Wrongs" clipboard. First, ask God to show you the sins you have committed. After you pray, write down those sins that come to mind. Take your time doing this. Remember, this is a private activity, so don't look at anyone else's board.

Give students time to pray and write. Encourage those who are not concentrating to pray and reflect. This may be difficult for some students. Also, make sure students do not look at each other's lists.

It's surprising how many sins come to mind when we pray. Sometimes we do wrong things and forget what we've done. Or we continue doing something and don't realize that God thinks what we're doing is wrong.

But God wants to cleanse these sins. Now I want you to pray again. This time, tell God that you know your sins are wrong and that you want Him to cleanse those sins from your life. Tell God about each sin separately, then erase that sin from your board. By the time you are finished praying, your board will be clean. The last thing to do is to thank God for forgiving all of your sins.

Give students time to follow your instructions.

Isn't it great that God is so forgiving? Sometimes it's hard to believe that He loves us that much. Let's memorize a verse that can help us remember to confess our sins all the time.

MEMORY VERSE ACTIVITY: Right Writings

1 John 1:9—"If we confess our sins, / he is faithful and just / and will forgive us our sins / and purify us from all unrighteousness."

Divide the verse into four parts as shown, and write them on four large strips of paper or posters.

Read the memory verse to the students. Then post the verse part as you talk about each one.

Let's look at the first part of this verse. It says "If we confess our sins." Who are we confessing to? *(God or Jesus.)* So we must first tell Jesus our wrongdoings. The next part says "he is faithful and just." This is telling us that God is fair and true and will listen to us. The third part is so important. It says He "will forgive us our sins." The last part, "and purify us from all unrighteousness," tells us that God will make us pure.

Let's play a game to learn this important verse. Take your clipboard and get ready to write. **Take down the four verse parts. Show the first one and read it to your students, then turn the poster over. Have the students write that verse part and hold up their clipboards. Check to see that they have written it correctly. Repeat with each verse part. Continue doing this until the verse is learned. Have the class say it together at the end. Listen to individuals repeat the verse if you have time.**

WEEKLY ASSIGNMENT: A Clean Slate

Optional Activity: Bring ribbon and craft magnets to class. Have students staple one end of a 12-inch length of ribbon to their clipboard and tie the other end to the marker. Then attach craft magnets to the back of the board so it can be put up on a metal surface.

Make sure students have their clipboards and markers. Take your "Record of Wrongs" clipboard home and use it every day. Follow the instructions at the top of the board. You don't have to wait until you have your board to confess your sins. As soon as you sin, confess it to God and ask Him to cleanse you and to give you the power to keep from doing this sin again. Then thank Him for forgiving you.

Sometimes we need to stop and ask God to reveal any sins to us that we forgot to confess or that we didn't realize we committed. Whenever you get a chance—perhaps during your daily time of prayer and reading your Bible—take time to write down the sins you have committed that you haven't confessed. Confess them to God and ask Him to cleanse you.

As you deal with your sin, your life will become more joyful and exciting. You will really experience the thrilling Christian adventure that God has for you.

Record of Wrongs

1. Take time to pray and ask God to show you the sins you have committed.
2. Write each sin as it comes to your mind.
3. Tell God you are sorry for each sin and ask Him to cleanse you.
4. Ask God to give you the power to keep from doing this sin.
5. Thank God for forgiving you.
6. Erase the sin to show that God has cleansed your heart.

Attitude Makes the Difference

Cut apart the situation cards.

1 Miguel and Jason are best friends. Jason's parents have a rule that he must attend boy's club at church but Miguel's parents allow him to stay home. Miguel wants Jason to skip boys' club at church to play video games with him. Jason tries to talk his parents into letting him stay home, but he knows their rule is that boys' club is too important to miss. Jason decides to...

2 Jasmine is the middle child in her family. She hates being the middle child because she thinks people don't pay as much attention to her as they do to her older brother and younger sister. Jasmine decides to take matters into her own hands. The next day she...

3 Robbie's stepmother is always trying to make him do things he doesn't like to do. One day, she tells him to wear a shirt that he hates. She is very firm about her decision. Robbie can't stand the shirt so he...

4 Chris got a new bicycle for his birthday. When he opens up the box, he sees a bike that he doesn't like. He wanted a better one. His parents have always told him to be thankful. But he doesn't feel thankful. Chris decides to...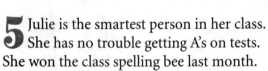

5 Julie is the smartest person in her class. She has no trouble getting A's on tests. She won the class spelling bee last month. Julie sits next to Lisa who has a hard time with math. Julie secretly thinks Lisa is stupid. When Lisa asks Julie a question about her math, Julie...

6 Matthew and Melissa are twins but they don't look alike. They are in different classes at school. Sometimes, Matthew is embarrassed about Melissa because she has to use crutches. At lunch, someone usually helps Melissa carry her things. But today, Melissa is trying to do it alone. Matthew meets her in the hall. She doesn't see him. He decides to...

The Great Battle

LESSON PLAN

OBJECTIVE: Students will learn about spiritual warfare and how to use the armor God has provided for the battle.

APPLICATION: Students will identify one personal problem situation and an appropriate piece of armor to use in that situation.

LESSON PLAN ELEMENT	ACTIVITY	TIME	SUPPLIES
Opening Activity	*A Tough Tissue*	7–10	Empty paper towel tube; rubber band; 2 sheets of double-ply facial tissue; sugar; wooden spoon; ruler
Bible Story—Ephesians 6:10–13, recognizing the armor of God	*Put On Your Armor*	10–15	Bible; 1 copy of the soldier and pieces of armor from "Battle Armor" handout; scissors; 1 copy of the "Enemies" handout
Check for Understanding	*Battle Check*	2–3	Drawings of pieces of armor from Bible Story
Memory Verse Activity	*Marching Orders*	3–5	
Lesson Activity	*Battlefield Training*	8–12	4 copies of "Battle Armor" handout; 1 copy each of "Battlefield Positions 1 and 2" handouts; 1 copy of "Enemies" handout; index cards; glue; pen; scissors
Application	*Wielding the Weapons*	7–10	Weapons used in the Battlefield Game; index cards; glue; pen or pencils
Weekly Assignment	*Armed for Action*	3–5	Cards from previous activity; pens or pencils

Picture for a moment a British soldier in the Revolutionary War. He and his fellow soldiers fought against the Colonial forces, who were brilliantly led by General George Washington. As the small Colonial army fought against the overwhelming, superior troops of England, they were miraculously victorious. Even so, several British soldiers refused to surrender. Although their commander had signed a treaty of surrender, they refused to admit their defeat and continued with guerrilla activity.

This is a portrait of the Christian life. We read in Colossians 1:13,14 that God has rescued us out of the darkness and gloom of Satan's kingdom. The Christian flag of victory has been raised; Satan has been defeated. Yet he hasn't given up. His spiritual guerrilla warfare continues as he tries to entice us to sin.

When we walk in the control and fullness of the Holy Spirit, we must be prepared for spiritual conflict. I am sure that dozens of times every day—at home, at work, at the grocery store, while driving on the freeway—you face temptations to compromise your Christian convictions. None of us in this life have gotten to the point of perfection.

Ephesians 6:10–18 exhorts us to "put on the full armor of God so that you can take your stand against the devil's schemes." Only by fighting with God's strength and by wearing His armor can we win the battle.

Your students are in just as much of a battle as you are. Many face a school culture that is determined to undermine many of the moral principles they have learned from God's Word. Others come from families where moral principles are questioned or ignored. Your preteen students are on the verge of developing mature bodies. As your students grow and develop, they will be increasingly tempted with fleshly desires. They need to know how to battle against wrong temptations. This lesson will help them understand the principles of spiritual warfare and the armor God has provided for them.

LESSON PLAN

OPENING ACTIVITY: A Tough Tissue

Discuss what happened when your students used their "Record of Wrongs" clipboard to confess their sins to God. Help students see how confession helped them in their attitudes and actions. Take time to thank God for His forgiveness.

You can do the Opening Activity either as a demonstration or in groups. If you do the activity in groups, you will need a set of materials for each group. Set out the tubes, wooden spoons, rubber bands, tissues, and sugar in different areas for each group to use. The groups will perform the activity as you explain it.

Read Ephesians 6:10. God wants us to be strong in Him. But often we try to do things without God. Let's do a demonstration to help us understand how we should fight against those who try to turn us away from God.

Let's say that this tube represents a Christian. This tissue will represent his new clean heart in Christ. Wrap the tissue around the end of the tube. Secure it with the rubber band. **If you are doing a demonstration, have a student do this.**

Read 1 Peter 5:8.

- Who does this verse say our enemy is? *(The devil.)*

Let's say that this wooden spoon represents the devil. He's always trying to pressure us to do what's wrong. Push the spoon handle into the tube. **The spoon handle will break through the tissue.** Satan tries many ways to push us into sinning. We cannot stand up against his pressure without God's help.

Now put a new tissue on the end of the tube and secure it with a rubber band. If you are doing a demonstration, have a student do this. This time, let's add some sugar to the tube to represent God and the godly armor He provides. God stands between us and the devil's pressure. **Pour about four inches of sugar into the tube.** Now let's see what happens when Satan pressures us to do wrong. **Put the spoon handle into the tube and press. The tissue will not break.** The tissue did not break! This demonstration helps us understand that God has provided us with protection. It is called the armor of God. We will learn about this in our Bible story.

BIBLE STORY: Put on Your Armor

Before Class: Make one copy of the "Battle Armor" handout and cut apart the pieces of the armor and the soldier. Have students sit in a circle. Pass the pieces of armor around the circle of students at the appropriate time.

Did you know that you are in the middle of a war right now? This war is between Satan and

God. Satan wants to defeat God. He tries to do this by attacking Christians and tempting them to do things that are against God's rules. We saw this in our demonstration with the broomstick.

The sad thing for Satan is that he has already lost the war. He doesn't want anyone to go to heaven, but he is not going to get his way. When Jesus died on the cross, He gained the victory in the war between Satan and God.

Although Satan knows that he has lost the war, he still tries to win battles. He and his many demons tempt Christians and unbelievers to do what's wrong.

Let's read some verses that explain this battle. **Read Ephesians 6:10–13.**

- According to these verses, who are Christians fighting against? *(The devil; powers of this dark world; spiritual forces of evil.)*

- What do we use to fight these evil forces? *(The armor of God.)*

We have three enemies. They are Satan, the world, and our fleshly desires. Let me read a verse about each enemy. **Read 1 Peter 5:8 (Satan). Read James 4:4 (the world). Read Galatians 5:16,17 (our sinful desires). Point out each picture from the "Enemies" handout as you explain each one.** Our enemies come at us all the time. They attack us through temptations. Satan and his demons tempt us to do all kinds of wrong things. The world makes sin look fun and exciting and pressures us to do these wrong things. Our sinful desires makes us want to do these temptations. All of these can be very powerful. We must always be on our guard.

During the days when Paul wrote this letter to the Ephesians, the Roman Empire ruled the known world. The Roman soldiers were known as brave, fierce fighters. They fought battles all over the world. They were well trained, and they carried the best armor available at that time. **Hold up the drawing of the soldier in his armor.** Let's look at the armor pieces that a soldier used.

Pass around the helmet. This helmet protected the Roman soldiers against wounds in the head. As you can see, it covered the soldier's head quite well.

Roman soldiers also had a piece of armor called the breastplate to protect their vital organs like the heart and lungs. **Pass around the breastplate.**

Roman soldiers wore a belt around their waist to keep their armor in place. This is what the belt looked like. **Pass around the belt.**

Soldiers did a lot of walking. Their feet needed to be protected, so the soldiers were outfitted with good shoes. **Pass the shoes around.**

The soldiers also carried something in each hand. In one hand, they carried a shield that protected them from incoming arrows or swords. **Pass around the shield.**

In the other hand, the soldiers carried their only weapon, a sword. This sword was not a long one that was hard to use. Instead, it was a short sword with a double-edged blade, meaning that it was sharp on both sides. The Roman soldiers could use this sword quickly and efficiently. It was a very effective weapon. **Pass around the sword.**

Paul wanted to explain to his readers all about spiritual warfare—the battle between Satan and his forces and God and His forces. Paul knew that his readers respected the fighting power of Roman soldiers, so he used them as his object lesson. What he was saying is that all believers all over the world make up God's army. Satan's army is the evil forces who want to defeat God's army. As a soldier in God's army, we use spiritual pieces of armor to protect ourselves and to defeat evil forces. Let's see how Paul described each piece of spiritual armor that we need for our spiritual battles.

A soldier would put on his armor before he even left for the battle. He never took them off while he was on the battlefield.

Pass around the helmet again. This is the helmet of salvation. When you asked Jesus to be your Savior, He promised to always protect you. You are a member of God's family. Your helmet of salvation will always protect you from blows from the devil, the world, and from your own evil desires.

Pass around the breastplate of righteousness. In our spiritual armor, this is called the breastplate of righteousness. Our righteousness is not our own efforts to do what's good; it is the righteousness we have because we are in God's army. We fight evil with right. Because we have God's righteousness and not our own, Satan cannot tell us that we aren't good enough for God's army. We stand for what's right—and God protects us.

Pass around the belt of truth. The Bible says that Satan is the father of lies. He hates the truth because God's truth is what defeats him. Our belt of truth is God's truth. The belt keeps the rest of our armor in place. God's truth will keep us from being deceived by Satan's lies. That's why it's so important for us to know God's truth.

Pass around the shoes of the gospel of peace. These are the shoes of the gospel of peace. A soldier's shoes are so important.

Our shoes take us places to tell others about Jesus. He is the Prince of Peace. He is the head of our army. As we tell others about the Prince of Peace, they too will become part of God's mighty army.

Pass around the shield of faith. A soldier takes up his shield when he sees that the enemy is ready to attack. Our shield protects us from unbelief. If you doubt God's promises, you aren't using your shield of faith. When you ask God to help you with something that you know is beyond your ability, you are using your shield of faith.

Pass around the sword of the Spirit. Our sword is God's Word, the Bible. It is very powerful against evil enemies and against our own sinful desires. When we read, memorize, study, and meditate on God's Word, we are taking action against our spiritual enemies. We break their power in our lives.

- Which piece of armor might help you in a situation you face right now? (*Allow students to describe their situation. Then help them decide which piece of armor would be most appropriate to use.*)

- What will happen if you don't use your armor? *(You will not be able to stand up against the devil. You will sin.)*

CHECK FOR UNDERSTANDING: Battle Check

Soldiers are drilled on their knowledge of their armor and the tactics for fighting. How well can you do in recognizing the armor you've been given to fight spiritual battles? **Hold up the drawing of each piece of armor and have a volunteer tell what it is and how it is used. Be sure your students know the appropriate name for each piece.**

How well can you recognize each enemy? **Hold up the drawing for each enemy and have a volunteer tell how that enemy attacks us.**

MEMORY VERSE ACTIVITY: Marching Orders

Ephesians 6:10,11—"Finally, be strong in the Lord and in his mighty power. Put on the full armor of God so that you can take your stand against the devil's schemes. For our struggle is not against flesh and blood, but against the rulers, against the authorities, against the powers of this dark world and against the spiritual forces of evil in the heavenly realms."

Write the verse on the board.

An important part of military life is learning to march. I'm sure you've seen soldiers marching in a parade or on review. We are members of God's army. As His soldiers, let's practice our marching as we say our memory verse.

> *Teaching Tip:* You may want to do this activity in a larger area such as a hallway, fellowship hall, or even outside. If so, write the verse on poster board.

Arrange students in at least two rows. Have them all face you. Repeat the verse together several times.

Explain the following marching orders. Use marching orders to repeat the verse. Have students stand at attention. Then have them march several steps in one direction, stand at attention, and repeat the verse in unison. Repeat commands as needed to learn the verse. When finished, have individual "soldiers" face the group and say the verse.

MARCHING ORDERS

Attention: Stand at attention with arms straight at your side

Hut, two, three, four: March in a certain direction in cadence

About face: Turn in the opposite direction

Halt: Stop

Left turn: turn left

Right turn: turn right

Repeat verse: say verse once

Parade rest: Relax with your hands behind your back

LESSON ACTIVITY: Battlefield Training

 Before Class: Make copies of the reproducible pages and create three kinds of cards, as shown below. When finished, you should have 61 cards.

- 20 "Battlefield Position" cards: Cut apart the situations from the "Battlefield Positions" reproducible and glue each to an index card.

- 32 "Battle Armor" cards: Cut apart the drawings from the "Battle Armor" reproducible and glue each to an index card. (Note: Each student will need a "helmet of salvation." If you have more than twelve students, either make two sets of cards and run two games at once or pair your students for the game.)

- 9 "Enemy" cards: Cut apart each enemy drawing from the "Enemy" reproducible and glue to an index card.

Rules of the Game:

1. **The goal is to win the most battles (have the most cards at the end of the game).**

2. **A player must draw a "helmet of salvation" card before he or she can collect any cards. This represents becoming a soldier by joining God's army at the time we became part of His family.**

3. **A player draws a card.**

- **If it is a "battle armor" card, the player lays the card in front of him or her.**

- **If it is an "enemy" card, the player must either quote the memory verse correctly or lose a turn. The card is discarded.**

- **If it is a "battlefield position" card, the player reads the card. If the player has that piece of armor, he or she keeps the "battlefield position" card. If not, the card is placed at the bottom of the draw pile.**

4. **The game is over when the last card is drawn and played.**

We're in a spiritual battle right now. When you're at home, at school, at church, shopping, or just playing, you are fighting to win. Let's play a game that will help us practice our spiritual battlefield tactics so we can win against our enemies. As we're playing, remember that it's only when we let God's Holy Spirit work in us that we will win the battle. He gives us the strength to use our armor.

Pick a number from 1 to 100. The student who gives the closest guess goes first. Have students sit in a circle around a table or on the floor. Explain the rules of the game. Then show each type of card and explain:

- The "battle armor" cards will help you win each battle. Use your battle armor cards to win battle position cards. **Show each type of "battle armor" card.**

- The "enemy" cards will cause you to lose a turn unless you can quote the memory verse. **Show each of the three types of "enemy" card.**

- The "battlefield position" cards explain one battle you might have to fight. To win the battle on the card, you must have the appropriate piece of armor. **Show an example of a "battlefield position" card.**

Mix the cards and place them in the center of your group.

Teaching Tip: If you have time, ask students what would happen if a person didn't use the armor in the situation given on the "battlefield position" cards.

Play the game until all cards are drawn and played or until time for this activity is over. Count the cards to find a winner. Applaud the winner.

APPLICATION: Wearing the Armor

Assemble the armor used previously in the game.

Now you can see that knowing about our spiritual armor is important for us in our daily lives. But it is not just knowing about it. We should also know when to use it.

For example, let's say you were taking a science test and didn't study for it. You can clearly see your classmate's paper. You are tempted to look at your classmate's answers.

- What piece of armor would you need in this situation? *(Belt of truth; other answers are acceptable if students have good reasons for using them.)*

You would need to call upon the Lord to help you stay truthful on your test and not cheat. Most of us have an area in our life in which we need extra help or protection. Maybe it is using bad language or getting angry. Think of an area that you might need help with. **Give students a moment to think.**

Set out the armor, glue, and pens or pencils. Now think of the spiritual armor that will help you with your area. Choose one of the pieces of armor and glue it onto an index card. Write your problem situation below the weapon. **Give students time to do this. Help those who may be unsure of what to write.**

WEEKLY ASSIGNMENT: Armed for Action

Now that you have chosen a piece of armor to work with this week on the area you chose, you are prepared for action. Take your card and turn it over. Make a chart that looks like this. **Draw the following chart on your chalkboard.**

DATE	ARMOR USED SUCCESSFULLY	DIDN'T USE WEAPON

Give students time to draw the chart on the back of their index cards.

Throughout the week, record the times you used your armor successfully and unsuccessfully. At the end of each day, praise God for your successes and confess your failures. Bring your card with you to our next lesson.

Let's close in prayer, asking God to help us this week. **Pray the following prayer or one of your own that addresses the particular spiritual warfare needs of your students.**

Dear God, help us to use your armor this week to fight off the attacks of Satan. In Jesus' name, amen.

If you are going on to the review session for your next class, ask students to bring a current picture of themselves that they can use for a cut-and-paste activity.

Battle Armor

Battlefield Positions 1

Battlefield Position: *Breastplate of righteousness*
You and your sister get identical new tennis shoes. You wear the same size. When you are playing, you scuff up your shoes. Hers still look brand new. You are tempted to trade shoes when she's not looking. But you know that's not right and might cause an argument. You do what's right by cleaning off your own shoes instead.

Battle Position: *Breastplate of righteousness*
Your mother gives you $5 to buy milk at the store. The milk costs only $3. Your mother forgets to ask you for the $2 in change. You want to buy some candy and soda with the money. You are tempted to keep the change but you know that wouldn't be honest or right. You give the money to your mother.

Battlefield Position: *Sword of the Spirit*

A new boy moves in next door. The first time you play together, he wins all the video games. You begin to dislike him because he always brags about winning. Then you remember Mark 12:31, "Love your neighbor as yourself." You use your Sword to help you love your new friend.

Battlefield Position: *Sword of the Spirit*

During the worship service at church, the choir sings a beautiful song about how wonderful God is. Then your pastor reads Psalm 92:1, "It is good to praise the LORD and make music to your name, O Most High." During the next song, you sing with your heart to praise God.

Battlefield Position: *Shield of faith*
Your grandmother is diagnosed with cancer. Your family is not sure she will live. You all pray about it, but you begin to wonder if God really cares. You put on your shield of faith by thanking God for caring about your family even when you don't feel like He does.

Battlefield Position: *Breastplate of righteousness*
Your mother goes to the store to buy groceries. You stay home alone. You turn on the TV and begin watching a music video with bad language. Then you remember that God wants you to look only at what's righteous and pure. You turn the TV to another show.

Battlefield Position: *Breastplate of righteousness*
A person at school tells you bad things about a classmate. You know no one else has heard this. You desperately want to tell your best friend the rumor. But you know that gossiping is wrong. You remember that the righteous thing to do is to love one another, so you don't tell anyone about the rumor.

Battlefield Position: *Sword of the Spirit*

In Sunday school, you memorize 1 Thessalonians 5:17, "Pray continually." When you get home, you learn that your parents might split up. You feel very sad and don't know what will happen to you. You use the verse to help you remember to talk to God about how you feel many times each day.

Battlefield Position: *Sword of the Spirit*

Your best friend gets a new dirt bike. You want his bike rather than your old, dented one. To help you control your feelings, you turn to Exodus 20:17 and read, "You shall not covet…anything that belongs to your neighbor." You remember that God wants you to be satisfied with what you have.

Battlefield Position: *Shield of faith*
You're afraid to be home alone at night. Your parents leave for a two-hour meeting. They give you their cell phone number but tell you to use it only in case of an emergency. You feel scared. Then you remember God promises to always be with you—even when you don't feel He's there. His promise makes your fear go away.

Battlefield Positions 2

Battlefield Position: *Shield of faith*
Your father has lost his job. The family's bills are not paid. Your parents call a family prayer time. You can see that your mother is very worried. But you remember that God promises to take care of His children. You encourage your mother with this fact.

Battlefield Position: *Shield of faith*
A boy from your school was killed in a car accident last week. You start thinking about how scary dying is. Sometimes, you feel afraid of what will happen to you if you die. Then you remember that you are God's special child. You know that He will take you to heaven when you die.

Battlefield Position: *Shoes of the gospel of peace*
Your class participates in a pen pal program with students from another country. Your pen pal writes about how her family does not believe in God. You write back and tell her how much Jesus means to you and how much He loves her. You also send her a Bible.

Battlefield Position: *Shoes of the gospel of peace*
You know that your grandparents do not believe in God. In your family, you pray for them to become Christians. When you are visiting your grandparents, you go for a drive with your grandfather. You tell him what you are learning in Sunday school, especially how much God loves him.

Battlefield Position: *Shoes of the gospel of peace*
You silently pray to thank God for your lunch at school. A friend notices you bowed your head. She asks what you were doing. At first, you think of an excuse to give her. But then you say you were praying to thank Jesus for all He has done for you. Then you explain how to become part of God's family.

Battlefield Position: *Shoes of the gospel of peace*
A new boy moves into the neighborhood. He does not go to church anywhere. You want him to know about God's love. You invite him to your church so you can help him find out about Jesus.

Battlefield Position: *Belt of truth*
A book your friend is reading says that the world happened by chance. It was not created. Your friend isn't sure about what to believe. You explain that God created everything and that God loves him.

Battlefield Position: *Belt of truth*
You accidentally scratched your friend's video game CD when he wasn't looking. Now it won't work properly. You put the CD back in the case and put the case away. You decide not to mention what you did. But then you put on the belt of truth and admit to him that you scratched his CD.

Battlefield Position: *Belt of truth*
You almost always get A's on your math tests. But today you forgot to study about fractions. You don't know several answers on your test so you look at your neighbor's paper. When you get your test back, you have an A and the answers you copied you got right. But you know that you don't deserve that grade. Even though it's hard, you go up and tell the teacher what you did.

Battlefield Position: *Belt of truth*
You go to the mall with your mother to buy three new shirts. You pay for them with money you saved from your allowance and for working. You walk outside. When you look at your receipt, you notice that you were charged for only two. The cashier made a mistake. That means you have money left over. After thinking a moment, you decide to go back and tell the cashier the truth.

Enemies

The Devil

The World

Our Sinful Desires

The Devil

The World

Our Sinful Desires

The Devil

The World

Our Sinful Desires

Passport to Adventure

LESSON PLAN

OBJECTIVE: Students will review the concept of living the abundant life in Christ.

APPLICATION: Students will learn how to continue progressing in their Christian adventure.

LESSON PLAN ELEMENT	ACTIVITY	TIME	SUPPLIES
Opening Activity	*Passport to the Christian Adventure*	7–10	Real passport; "Christian Adventure Passport" handouts; students' current pictures; a date stamp and pad; pine-green construction paper; scissors; markers; pencils or pens; glue
Bible Story—Assorted Scriptures from the life of Jesus; the disciples travel with Jesus	*The Lifetime Journey*	10–15	Bibles; "Passports"; map of Palestine during Jesus' time; map markers (see activity); paper; pencils; stamp and pad
Memory Verse Activity	*Words to Walk By*	3–5	Construction paper; marker
Lesson Activity	*Taking the Essentials*	8–12	"Passports"; pencils; stamp and pad
Application	*One More Stop*	7–10	"Passports"; pencils, stamp and pad
Check for Understanding	*Stop, Stop, Stop, Stop!*	2–3	"Passports"
Weekly Assignment	*Keep On Going*	3–5	"Passports"; pencils

LESSON INTRODUCTION

Alex was distressed over his constant failure to live the Christian life victoriously. "I'm always failing," he said. "I know what is right, but I'm simply not able to keep the many commitments, resolutions, and dedications that I make to the Lord almost daily.

"What's wrong with me? Why do I constantly fail? How can I push that magic button that will change my life and make me the kind of person God wants me to be and the kind of person I want to be?"

All of us experience this conflict when we walk in our own strength. But the victory is ours as we learn to abide in Christ.

Jesus said, "I am the vine, you are the branches. He who abides in Me, and I in him, bears much fruit; for without Me you can do nothing" (John 15:5, NKJ). The reality of abiding in Christ and Christ abiding in us is made possible through the indwelling Holy Spirit.

Abiding in Christ means to be one with Him by faith. It is to live in conscious dependence upon Him, recognizing that it is His life, His power, His wisdom, His strength, and His ability operating through us that enable us to live according to His will. We do this by surrendering the throne of our lives to Him and by faith drawing upon His resources to live a supernatural, holy life.

The "abiding life"—we in Christ, He in us—enables us to live a victorious and fruitful life. Millions of Christians throughout the world profess their love for Christ each week by attending church services, singing songs, studying their Bibles, and attending prayer meetings. Yet, all the talk in the world will never convince anyone that you or I truly love the Lord unless we obey Him, and this includes bearing fruit for Him. The only way we can demonstrate that we are truly abiding in Him is to produce fruit, which involves introducing others to our Savior as well as living holy lives.

Living the Christian adventure brings lasting joy. "I have told you this," Jesus said, "so that my joy may be in you and that your joy may be complete" (John 15:11).

To live this adventure, we must learn to live in Christ, constantly yielding total control of our lives to Him.

In this review lesson, your students will begin by recalling Christ's sacrifice for us and how important it is to know Him personally. That is the first step to the Christian adventure.

Your students will also review other steps in the Christian adventure—offering yourself to God; counting yourself dead to sin; and obeying God. As you discuss the key concepts of the study, allow students to express their problems in living the Christian life. Help them apply what they have learned to their most difficult situations.

LESSON PLAN

DING! DONG!

OPENING ACTIVITY: Passport to the Christian Adventure

 Before Class: Find someone who has a passport that you can show to the class. Cut construction paper in half for passport covers.

Allow students to share what happened during the last week when they used their piece of spiritual armor. Help students see the difference that spiritual armor makes in our lives.

 Optional Activity: If you have access to a Polaroid camera, take your students' pictures for the passport activity.

Begin this lesson by holding up the closed passport.

• Do you know what this is? *(A passport.)*

• What is it used for? *(To identify you as you travel to other countries throughout the world.)*

Let's look inside to see what information it holds. **Open the passport and point out each element inside as you talk about it.** It has a person's legal name, date of birth, and description. It also has a picture of the person. Here is an area to record when and where the person has been. The customs office at the border of a country will stamp the passport here to let the person enter the country. **If the passport has stamps from other countries, discuss where the person has traveled.**

Pass out the "Christian Adventure Passport" handouts, construction paper, scissors, markers, pencils or pens, and glue. Today, we will make passports to represent the journey we are taking with Jesus through life.

Have students fold construction paper in half. Cut apart pages on handouts. (Leave pages 1–2 and 3–4 connected.) Fold pages 1–2 and 3–4 along the middle. Glue page 1 to back of construction paper book front cover and page 4 to the back cover. Glue pages 2 and 3 together to complete the booklet. With markers, write "Passport" on the front cover.

In the last twelve lessons, we learned many things we do on our journey that makes it an adventure. We learned about the power that Jesus has to help us on our journey through life. We discovered the wonderful ways we have of communicating with God—through prayer and our Bible. We also practiced ways God has given us to defeat the sin in our lives and to produce the fruit of good deeds. When we live in Christ's power, we will have adventures we could never have any other way.

When you apply for a passport, someone in the government signs it to make sure it is legal. He validates your passport. We might say we also get a validated passport in our Christian life. When we ask Jesus to be our Savior, we become part of His family. We begin the Christian adventure that He has planned for us. It's as if He gives us our passport and validates it for us. He tells God the Father that we are truly part of God's family because He has paid for our sins in full.

Let's fill out our passports for our Christian adventure. Print your name, date of birth, and other information. Glue your picture in the square. **Give students time to do this.**

To begin the Christian adventure, you must make sure Jesus is your personal Savior. We have talked a lot about this, but perhaps someone here has not made this decision. If you haven't, see me after class.

Turn to page 2. On the blank lines, write when you made the decision to follow Christ. **Give students time to do this. Circulate and help those who may be uncertain of when they made this decision or those who may not have made this decision. Make sure you have material prepared so you can deal with any student who seems unsure about his or her status in God's family.**

Passport pictures are stamped so that someone else's picture cannot be substituted on the passport. The stamp won't match up with a different picture. We can stamp our passport picture because we know that our passport to heaven cannot be used by anyone else. It is ours alone. **Use your stamper to stamp the date on the passport over the picture with the stamp halfway off the picture.**

When everyone has finished, say: Take your passport with you to the Bible Story time, which is your first stop on your journey with Jesus.

BIBLE STORY: The Lifetime Journey

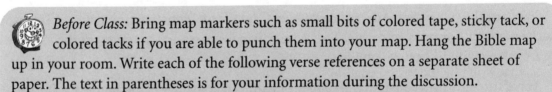

Before Class: Bring map markers such as small bits of colored tape, sticky tack, or colored tacks if you are able to punch them into your map. Hang the Bible map up in your room. Write each of the following verse references on a separate sheet of paper. The text in parentheses is for your information during the discussion.

- Matthew 4:18–24 *(around the Sea of Galilee; calling His disciples and teaching people)*
- Matthew 24:1–8 *(at the temple in Jerusalem; telling about the future, prophesying)*
- Mark 2:1–12 *(Capernaum; healing and teaching)*
- Luke 19:1–10 *(Jericho; to tell Zacchaeus about God)*
- John 6:1–14 *(Tiberias; taught the people and fed them)*
- John 11:1,38–44 *(Bethany; to raise Lazarus from the dead)*

Tell me about a trip you've been on. It could be short like a field trip at school, a day trip with your family, or a longer trip of a week or two. **Allow students to share their experiences. Emphasize the types of vehicles used, types of places visited, and the number of people traveling together.**

Now imagine that you were traveling with Jesus while He was on earth.

- How would that be different than the trips you have been on? (*Jesus had to walk, not ride in cars or on airplanes. Jesus couldn't stay in hotels. Jesus didn't have a good home to come back to whenever He wanted to rest.*)

- Why did Jesus take so many trips in His lifetime? (*He wanted to talk to as many people as He could. He had a lot of important things to do. He wanted to show His disciples lots of things.*)

- Why was Jesus always around so many people? (*People wanted to see Him. He loved people. He was training His disciples, so they were always with Him.*)

Jesus was always on the go. He traveled from city to city, talking to people and teaching them what God wanted them to know. Let's look at some of the places He went and why He went there.

Divide students into six groups. (A group could be one person.) Give each group one of the sheets of paper with a reference written on it and a pencil. Make sure each group has a Bible. I have given each group a reference to look up and read. Assign one person in your group to do this. In the passage, find the name of the place Jesus traveled to and why He went there. Write your answers on your paper.

Give groups time to work. Then have one person from each group come up to the map, mark the place mentioned in their passage, and explain why Jesus traveled there.

When we go places, we usually are taking a trip or doing something fun. Jesus made trips to help people and to do the will of God, His Father.

- In the passage you read in your group, how was Jesus doing the will of the Father? (*Taking care of people; telling people about God; teaching His disciples so that they could do what He did after He went back to heaven; telling people what will happen in the future so they can be prepared.*)

The real adventure is knowing Jesus and living the life God has planned for us. Many times, that won't be the easiest road to take, but it will be the most wonderful.

- How did the disciples get to know Jesus? (*They talked to Him. They spent lots of time with Him. They watched what He did.*)

- We can't talk to Jesus face to face, but what are some ways we get to know God? (*We read the Bible and learn about God. We pray and talk to Him. We hear sermons and Sunday school lessons about Jesus.*)

Knowing God is the first stop on our journey with Jesus. On your passport, write "knowing God" under the 1st Stop. **Give students time to write.** Getting to know God and Jesus will take a lifetime. But it will be an exciting part of your Christian adventure.

Before we go on to our next stop, let's learn a verse that tells us how great our Christian adventure will be.

MEMORY VERSE ACTIVITY: Words to Walk By

John 10:10—"I have come that they may have life, and have it to the full."

> *Before Class:* Cut out fifteen footprints from construction paper. Write one word of John 10:10 on each footprint. The reference should go on one footprint. Before this activity, set out the footprints on the floor in order, spacing them so the students can walk on them.

Have the class read the verse together. Jesus wanted our walk with Him to be full of abundance. This means that He wants your life to be fully connected to Him and to be filled with joy.

Let's learn this verse by walking. Each word of the verse is written on one footprint. This reminds us of our walk with Jesus. I am going to ask one of you to walk on the footprints and read each word as you go.

Have one student walk on the footprints. Then have him or her choose one footprint to turn over. Now choose a second student to walk and recite the verse, including the missing word. Repeat this process until all the footprints have been turned down.

Have the students write the verse under the 1st Stop. See if they can write the verse without turning up the footprints. Then have students come up individually and say the verse to you. As they do, stamp the date under the 1st Stop.

Say the verse together to close. Then go on to the 2nd Stop.

LESSON ACTIVITY: Taking the Essentials

Gather students in a circle.

- What are some things you must take with you on a trip? *(Clothes; suitcases; money; food; map.)*

These items help us survive our trip and make it more pleasant. This is also true of our journey with Jesus. We need to make sure we have some things with us to have a successful journey. If you remember in our previous lessons, we talked about the throne or control center of our lives.

- Who should be sitting on this throne? *(Jesus.)*

- What does it mean to have Jesus on the throne of our life? *(That Jesus is in control of every area of my life.)*

Open your passport. Under the 2nd Stop, draw a throne with Jesus on it. **Give students time to draw the throne.**

This is the second stop on our journey—offering ourselves to God. We can do this only if we ask Jesus to be on the throne of our lives. Right now, ask Him to take over your life. We have talked about this step before. We must give over every part of our lives—our belongings, our actions, our talents. Everything we have, we must give to Him. He will help you make your life into a miracle. I'll give you a few moments to pray. You can pray something like this: "Dear heavenly Father, I want to give you control of everything in my life. (At this point, list some things you want to give to Him.) I thank You for loving me so much and for taking care of my life. In Jesus' name, amen."

Give students a few moments to pray silently. Then have them write "offering myself to God" under the 2nd Stop. Allow the students to stamp this stop.

Now let's go on to our next stop, which has to do with sin.

- What should you do if you sin? *(Confess my sin to God.)*

Confessing sin helps us stay on the right track. If you have ever been hiking in the wilderness, you know how important it is to keep on the path. You might get lost, get into some poison ivy, or even hurt yourself in the brush. That's a picture of what happens to us when we sin. We get off God's path and into dangerous territory.

I'm going to give you a chance to confess your sin right now. It's very important to tell God about what you do wrong as soon as you do it. It's like getting something disgusting spilled on your clothes. You want to get it off right away. Sin is disgusting. We need to get rid of it right away by confessing it to God.

I'm going to give you a minute to talk to God and confess your sin. First, ask God to show you the sins you haven't confessed to Him. Whatever He brings to your mind you need to confess.

Pray something like this: "Dear heavenly Father, please show me what I have done wrong that I need to confess to you." Wait a few seconds to see what comes into your mind. Then continue praying like this: "I am sorry that I did this sin." Be sure to name your sin. God knows what you did but He wants you to tell Him. Then pray: "Help me keep from sinning this way again. Thank You so much for forgiving my sin. In Jesus' name, amen."

Give students time to reflect and pray.

Open your passport and write "confessing my sin" under the 3rd Stop. Then stamp it. **Give students time to do this.**

- In our Christian walk, there are two other things we should do everyday. What are they? *(Read my Bible and pray.)*

Both of these help us to get guidance from God, our leader. We have already made a couple of stops to pray. Now let's talk about reading the Bible. It is our map for our Christian adventure. How can we travel on our journey without our map? We would get lost. But the Bible keeps us on the right track.

At various times in our journey, we have to stop and read our map. Let's do this right now. **Have students look up Matthew 4:19 in their Bibles.**

- What is the greatest thing we can do on our Christian adventure? *(Follow Jesus.)*

with my mother." Write what you thought of in your passport. **Give students time to think and write.**

When you use your passport, follow this pattern. First go through Stops 1 through 3 to make sure that your heart is right with God. Then act on the Stop you are working on. Ask God to help you obey Him in the area you wrote down. If you are successful in obeying God, write a date on that Stop. Just as you can travel to the same foreign country more than once, you can go to each Stop more than once. Each time you do, write in a new date.

This is the last lesson in our journey to learn about the Christian adventure. We have learned a lot about who Jesus is and how He helps us live. We truly are on an adventure with Jesus. It will last the rest of our lives!

Thank your students for the privilege of teaching them throughout this series. Then pray for them, mentioning some of the things that God can help them with over the next few weeks.

If you are going on to the next book, *Discovering Our Awesome God,* introduce the book by mentioning some of the exciting things that the class will be doing.

Christian Adventure Passport

1

Heavenly Passport

Picture

Surname (last name) _____

Given name _____

Date of birth _____

Sex _____ Place of birth _____

Date of issue _____

_____

2

The Ruler of the Universe, Jesus Christ, hereby requests that all who are concerned may know that this passport permits citizen to pass without hindrance or delay or in case of need to give all lawful aid and protection to this person.

I decided to follow Christ on:

_____
DATE

_____
SIGNATURE

3

1st Stop

2nd Stop

3rd Stop

4

4th Stop

5th Stop

6th Stop

THE GOOD NEWS GLOVE
Bill Bright
(ISBN 1-56399-074-1)

A classic and fun witnessing tool, this colorful glove helps children understand and remember the gospel. Each finger communicates a basic spiritual truth in an exciting, game-like fashion that captures kids' attention and hearts. Use it alone or with *The Good News Comic*.

IN SEARCH OF THE GREATEST TREASURE
Bill Bright
(ISBN 1-56399-120-9)

Join a delightful band of children as they embark on a treasure hunt…not for buried treasure, but for the greatest person who ever lived. Written in comic-book fashion, this brightly-colored, easy-to-use booklet helps children understand who Jesus is and why He is the Greatest Treasure.

A CHILD OF THE KING
Bill Bright and Marion R. Wells
(ISBN 1-56399-150-0)

A Child of the King is a timeless tale of a kingdom turned away from the sun, a brave but vulnerable orphan, a diabolical foe and a king whose love never ends. The story could be your own. Perhaps it is.

Written in the beloved, allegorical tradition of C. S. Lewis' *Chronicles of Narnia* and J. R. R. Tolkien's *The Lord of the Rings*, *A Child of the King* takes you on a quest for truth, virtue, and self-worth in a dark and hostile world. Share the adventures of Jotham, the People of the Book, and others in the Kingdom of Withershins…and realize your own high calling as a child of the King.

TEN BASIC STEPS TOWARD CHRISTIAN MATURITY
Bill Bright

These time-tested Bible studies offer a simple way to understand the basics of the Christian faith and provide believers with a solid foundation for growth. The product of many years of extensive development, the studies have been used by thousands. Leader's and Study Guides are available.

Introduction: The Uniqueness of Jesus

Step 1: The Christian Adventure

Step 2: The Christian and the Abundant Life

Step 3: The Christian and the Holy Spirit

Step 4: The Christian and Prayer

Step 5: The Christian and the Bible

A HANDBOOK FOR CHRISTIAN MATURITY
Bill Bright
(ISBN 1-56399-040-7)

This book combines the *Ten Basic Steps* Study Guides in one handy volume. The lessons can be used for daily devotions or with groups of all sizes.

TEN BASIC STEPS LEADER'S GUIDE
Bill Bright
(ISBN 1-56399-028-8)

This book contains teacher's helps for the entire *Ten Basic Steps* Bible Study series. The lessons include opening and closing prayers, objectives, discussion starters, and suggested answers to the questions.

> These and other fine products from *NewLife* Publications are available from your favorite bookseller or by calling (800) 235-7255 (within U.S.) or (407) 826-2145, or by visiting www.newlifepubs.com.

Certificate

This certificate is awarded to:

_____

for successfully completing "Beginning the Christian Adventure,"
Book 1 of the Children's Discipleship Series

_____
CHURCH AND CITY

_____
DATE

_____
NAME, POSITION

_____
NAME, POSITION